Lily pulled back, staring at him in open disbelief.

She had the power to arouse a man like Carter?

For a reasonably intelligent woman, her brain was taking an inordinately long time wrapping itself around this new concept of being sexy to someone.

But she liked the idea. A lot.

It dawned on her that she wanted to drive this man out of his mind sexually possibly worse than anything else she'd ever wanted.

"Once I'm safely inside your precious military base, can we continue this?" she asked in a breathless voice.

"Oh, we'll continue this, all right. I know better than to walk away from your kind of fire, *chère.*"

"Promise?"

★ ★ ★

D0035105

Dear Reader,

Often readers ask me where I get the ideas for my books. Sometimes, they're pure imagination. But now and then, I find inspiration for my stories from the news, and this book happens to be one of those. The Doomsday device featured in this book is, in fact, believed to exist. And that led me to the inevitable question of, what would happen if something accidentally triggered it? And voilà, this book was born.

That, and the thought of an astrophysicist and a soldier falling in love was just too much fun to resist. Of course, it doesn't hurt that my minor in college was subatomic particle physics, and I went on to become a soldier after college! I suspect I was never as clever as Dr. Lily James, and I know I was never as cool as Carter Baigneaux, but they're still especially near and dear to my heart.

So pull up a lawn chair on a dark and starry night, gaze out into the romantic grandeur of the cosmos and get ready for danger as we embark on our next H.O.T. Watch mission…this time to save the world.

Happy reading!

Cindy Dees

CINDY DEES

Soldier's Night Mission

ROMANTIC
SUSPENSE

This book is dedicated to every dreamer who's ever gazed out into the night sky and wondered if we're not alone in the universe.

 SILHOUETTE BOOKS

Recycling programs
for this product may
not exist in your area.

ISBN-13: 978-0-373-27719-3

SOLDIER'S NIGHT MISSION

Selected Books by Cindy Dees

CINDY DEES

started flying airplanes while sitting in her dad's lap at the age of three and got a pilot's license before she got a driver's license. At age fifteen, she dropped out of high school and left the horse farm in Michigan, where she grew up, to attend the University of Michigan. After earning a degree in Russian and East European Studies, she joined the U.S. Air Force and became the youngest female pilot in its history. She flew supersonic jets, VIP airlift and the C-5 Galaxy, the world's largest airplane. During her military career, she traveled to forty countries on five continents, was detained by the KGB and East German secret police, got shot at, flew in the first Gulf War and amassed a lifetime's worth of war stories.

This RITA® Award-winning author's first book was published in 2002 and since then she has published over twenty-five bestselling and award-winning novels. She loves to hear from readers and can be contacted at www.cindydees.com.

Dear Reader,

Yes, it's true. We're changing our name! After over twenty-five years of being part of Harlequin Enterprises, Silhouette Books will officially seal the merger by taking the company's name.

So if you notice a few changes on the covers starting April 2011—Silhouette Special Edition becoming Harlequin Special Edition, Silhouette Desire becoming Harlequin Desire and Silhouette Romantic Suspense becoming Harlequin Romantic Suspense—don't be concerned.

We'll continue to have the same fantastic authors, wonderful stories, eye-catching covers and emotional, compelling reads. We're just going to be moving under the overall company name, which will make us even easier for you to see in the stores, on the internet, and wherever you usually find us!

So look for the new logo, but remember, beneath the image will be the same promise of romantic stories of love, passion, adventure, family and a whole lot more. Just the way you like them!

Sincerely,

The Editors at Harlequin Books

Chapter 1

Carter Baigneaux shifted uncomfortably in the auditorium-style seat. Being back in a college classroom felt like some sort of weird time warp. Several hundred students in front of him squirmed in their seats, too. Although given how hot the professor was, he figured their squirming had more to do with hormones than flashbacks.

The lecturer was Lily James. From up here she looked waiflike and fragile and impossibly young to be a Dr. James, assistant professor of astronomy at a major university. Or maybe he was just getting old. Lord knew he felt ancient sitting among these pimply teenagers. Who knew the long-haired, tie-dyed hippie craze was on its way back in? It didn't help that his hair was cut in a military buzz and his shirt was crisply starched. At least no one had called him a pig or railed at him about the system yet.

Professor James said something about a quiz and a collective groan went up around him. Her sweet voice announced over the loud speakers, "I'll see you next Tuesday. Don't be late. You'll need the whole hour to get through the test."

The students around him surged out of their seats. Anticipation quickened his gut. He was looking forward to meeting the young professor up close and personal. Just how attractive was she at arm's length? Carter moved into the aisle to make his way down to the long lab table stretching across the lecture hall. But he'd failed to take into account the flood of students rushing up and out of the double doors behind him, and he floundered like a salmon trying to make its way upstream to spawn.

He looked over the sea of heads sweeping toward him and saw Dr. James stuffing her lecture notes into a leather satchel. Dodging and weaving, he progressed only a few rows toward her before she slung the bag over her shoulder and turned to her right. She was heading for a door behind the podium marked Staff Only. He pushed harder, and only succeeded in making a bunch of students complain at him. Screw this. He stepped into an empty row and threw his leg over the seats into the next row. Descending awkwardly over the rows of seats, he made his way to the front of the auditorium. But he wasn't fast enough. She'd disappeared.

The door she'd used led to a storeroom crammed with supplies for science experiments. He looked left and right. There. A red exit sign. He dashed to the door and shoved it open. A glare of sunshine blinded him, and he squinted across the parklike expanse of grass before him. Hundreds of students crisscrossed it, hurrying to and from classes. Where was the petite frame and long brunette locks of his quarry? He thought he spotted her and took off running.

His thigh muscles twinged warningly. *Not now, dammit!* He wasn't even in combat. There was no reason for them to lock up. Concentrating hard on keeping Dr. James in sight and reminding himself continuously he was merely jogging across a college campus, he managed to keep moving, to stay functional.

She might be walking, but she was moving at a brisk pace, forcing him to run at a good clip to catch up to her. He pulled close enough to see that he had, indeed, spotted the right woman. But a street loomed ahead, lined with parked cars. If she'd driven here, she could get into her vehicle and be gone before he could get her attention and speak with her. Irritated, he put on a burst of speed that sent his entire body twitching in a threatening seize-up. *Not. Now.*

She turned toward the street as if to cross it. "Dr. James!" he called.

She slowed down. Started to turn her head toward him. That was when he registered the van sitting at a stop sign across the street. It surged forward and swung around the corner, pulling to a stop directly in front of Lily. The side door of the van slid open and two men leaped out in a jerky, stop-action sequence.

Two things happened simultaneously in Carter's head. First, he swore—violently. And second, time shifted into distorted slow motion around him. He sprinted toward the professor full-out. The men ducked between the parked cars as Carter launched himself toward the professor in a desperate bid to keep her out of their clutches.

Impact. He slammed into Lily James, who was every bit as slender as she'd seemed, just as the first man reached out for her. Carter's momentum sent her flying beneath him and he clutched her close as he twisted in midair like a cat. He crashed, back first, to the ground, the concrete sidewalk knocking the wind out of him and sending time rushing forward to normal speed all at once.

"What the—" Lily gasped, the wind knocked out of her as well.

The first man's arms closed on empty air as the second would-be assailant smashed into him from behind. The two men staggered as Carter rolled, depositing Lily on the ground before leaping to his feet.

Snarling, he stalked toward the two assailants as they untangled themselves and simultaneously spotted the large, angry man advancing on them. And he wasn't alone. Passersby were gathering quickly, buzzing with consternation. The men whirled as one and raced for the van. They dived into its dark interior and the vehicle peeled out, tires screeching, and turned the corner. Who in the hell were *they?* And why had they just tried to kidnap Lily James? He knew good and well why the U.S. government wanted to talk to her, but what did these jokers want with her?

Carter caught the license plate and memorized it as he turned to check on the woman he'd just laid a killer tackle on. A crowd of people had already gathered around the spot where she'd gone down, and panic kicked him in the gut. What if he'd seriously hurt her?

The same crowd that had chased off the other men was turning on him now. What? They thought he was one of the bad guys? But he'd kept her out of their clutches!

"I stopped them—" he started. A man grabbed his upper arm. "The campus police are on the way, young man."

Dammit. He *needed* to talk to her. But he also emphatically did not need to make a scene about it. Although he supposed he'd already blown that right out of the water with his spectacular flying tackle.

He watched, frustrated, as someone assisted Dr. James to her feet.

"Dr. James!"

She glanced back over her shoulder in his direction and made eye contact with him. Lights exploded behind his eyes and his body felt as if it had been struck by lightning. Her dark, huge eyes pierced him accusingly until his very soul bled. Aw, crap. He'd terrified the poor woman. And then she was gone, someone's arm looped solicitously around her shoulder, leading her away.

More people closed in on him, demanding, questioning. "I was only trying to help—"

But the crowd wasn't in much of a mood to listen. Maybe the campus police would be calmer. A quiet call to his headquarters to verify his identity, a quick statement explaining how he'd saved the professor—not assaulted her—and he'd be cut loose. He hoped.

But in the meantime, Lily James was gone. The crowd thought he was one of her attackers. The van was *long* gone. And worst of all, he'd totally screwed up the first operational mission he'd been given since…well, since. Disgust rolled through him like acid. All he had to do was find a woman on a nice, safe college campus and talk to her, for God's sake. And he couldn't even pull that off.

He closed his eyes and prayed for the earth to swallow him whole. No such luck. The people around him began to make increasingly radical and ugly comments, and he was actually relieved when the campus police arrived and escorted him to a squad car.

His supervisors at H.O.T. Watch headquarters were going to kill him. The Hunter Operations Teams that ran out of the supersecret facility were not in the habit of failing in their missions. And as of now, a serious national security problem was going unsolved because he couldn't manage to find and talk to one lousy scientist.

Not to mention he was deeply alarmed by his near freeze-up back there. If he couldn't overcome his humiliating affliction, and soon, he was well and truly done as a Special Forces operator. Any dreams he'd ever harbored of getting back out into the field would be irrevocably smashed to smithereens by a brown-eyed assistant professor of astronomy.

Lily James paced her living room, eyeing the sky outside out of long habit. The night was clear and crisp, the heavens dusted with twinkling stars just begging her to come out and play. And on any other night she would have packed up her gear, driven out into the desert and done just that, spending the entire night gazing up into their fathomless wonder, imagining who might be out there gazing back at her.

Except today, a bunch of guys had tried to kidnap her and, had the biggest attacker of the three not knocked himself silly by tackling her like a madman, they might have succeeded. The walls of her house were closing in on her, suffocating her by slow degrees. But for once, she didn't run from the claustrophobia. For once, it felt safe to be trapped inside, locked in this little box.

Not that it was a bad room. Her books lined two walls from floor to ceiling. The sofa was a sloppy, down-stuffed affair perfect for stretching out on to read or take a nap. She had a nice flat-screen TV, a combined Christmas/birthday gift from her parents last year, but she didn't watch it often.

And then, of course, there was the huge skylight in the ceiling that opened up to her beloved skies. It had been a royal pain finding a contractor who would install an actual window in her roof, but she didn't want the view distorted by a domed skylight. It was nearly the size of a double plate-glass door, and she could see a substantial chunk of the northern hemisphere through it while lying on her sofa.

The phone rang and she checked the caller ID to see who it was. Ugh. She didn't feel like talking to her mother tonight. Her parents had, understandably, been deeply alarmed when she'd told them of the attack upon her. But then, in their usual hopelessly intellectual fashion, they'd rationalized the whole thing as some sort of misguided student prank.

Lily rejected the notion. She'd seen the looks in those men's eyes. They'd been dead serious and had emphatically not been students. But her parents lived in their own clueless bubble, safe from reality, and she knew better than to try to change their minds. Sometimes she wondered if they'd both done just a little too much LSD in the sixties and fried a few too many mental circuits.

She headed for the sofa to lie down and stargaze when a new noise stopped her in her tracks. Who could be at her door at this hour? She didn't have the kind of friends who would come over to check on her after her harrowing experience. Not only were most of them online buddies, but they were hardcore scientists who tended to run a little thin in the sympathy department.

Frowning, she moved over to the front door. "Who is it?" she called through the panel.

"My name is Carter Baigneaux, Dr. James. I work for the United States government and I need to speak with you."

The U.S. government? What could they want with her? Were the stories about extraterrestrials hidden away in government facilities true after all? Maybe they'd seen her paper on what aliens might look like and needed help analyzing one. Or maybe they'd received a transmission of some kind. She was an expert in radio signal analysis, her current work in superfast intergalactic particle smashing notwithstanding. Or maybe—

"Dr. James? Are you still there? If you'll open the door, I can show you my identification."

Oh. Right. Let the government man in so he could tell her what was going on. She unlocked both of the dead bolts and threw open the door. She recognized the big man instantly from his earlier tackle and tried to slam the door shut. But he was too fast and shoved a foot into the doorway. Even though he grunted as she slammed the door on his shoe, he didn't withdraw the block.

"Dr. James. I really am a government agent. Here. Let me pass my ID card to you. I swear I'm not going to hurt you."

She leaned against the door with all her weight—which wouldn't do a lick of good if the giant on the other side decided to shove back. Her heart slammed against her ribs in panic. What to do? If she quit pushing, the door would fly open and he'd be on her in a second. Her cell phone was on the coffee table halfway across the room. Should she make a jump for it and try to dial 911 before he caught her?

But she wasn't on campus, now. The local police would take several minutes to get here. Plenty of time for her attacker to drag her out of the house and into his van. She didn't stand a chance of overpowering him. The guy had to be at least six foot four. And it didn't take an astrophysicist to see he was seriously buff.

As she frantically tried, and failed, to come up with a plan, a white-and-green plastic card poked through the narrow opening in front of her nose. She stared at it as she continued to push with all her might against the door. Captain Carter Baigneaux. United States Army. She noted his date of birth—he was thirty-three years old. Brown hair.

Blue eyes. Cute picture. Okay, not cute exactly. Handsome and all-American were more precise descriptors. But neither of those captured the sheer physical power and intimidation factor of the man.

Still. He was in the army? Why did the army need to talk with her? She pushed a little less urgently against his foot. "What do you want?" she demanded. Rats. Her voice sounded all squeaky and terrified. No help for it. She *was* terrified.

"To talk, ma'am. Just to talk."

"About what?"

"Your work, ma'am. You may have discovered something of interest to us."

"Us who?"

"I already told you. I work for the government. It's classified, and I can't exactly yell about it while standing on your front porch."

"Why did the government try to kidnap me, then? They could've just asked me about my work. I'd have told them."

"The government did not try to kidnap you, ma'am."

"Then what would you call having three men run after me and try to jump on me and throw me into a van? As I recall, you physically leaped on me and knocked me to the ground. I'd call that an attack. Why on earth would I let you into my house?"

"Attacked—I saved you! Those men in the van were not with me. They were trying to assault you or kidnap you, and I stopped them!"

"Funny way you have of saving me. I've got a bunch of big ol' bruises to show for it."

"Yeah, well, I've got a few bruises to show for it myself."

"Do they hurt?" she demanded.

"As a matter of fact, they do," he answered a little sourly.

"Good."

A sigh wafted through the crack. "Ma'am, I messed up this afternoon, but I really do need to speak with you. I'm sorry if I scared you earlier. That was not my intent. I truly was trying to save you from those men in the van."

She replayed the events of the afternoon in her head. Was it possible this man was telling the truth? Someone behind her had called her name. That was just before a squeal of tires captured her attention. And then the big man—Carter Baigneaux—was rushing her in a blur from her left. The other two men came out of the van from directly in front of her.

Hmm. The two attacks had definitely come from different directions. And why would one man follow her on foot when the other two came out of the van? Why not just have all three men charge her from the van? Had Carter not knocked her down, the first two men would have had no trouble snatching her.

"Did you call out my name?" she asked.

"Yes. That was me. I wanted you to slow down so I could talk to you. You left your class out the storeroom door too fast for me to catch you any sooner to ask to speak with you. I had to chase you all the way across that grassy area."

Okay, so he'd been in her class and not with the other men in the van. His story might be true, after all.

"Tell you what, ma'am. Call the campus police. They ran my ID this afternoon and verified who I am and who I work for. I'll wait out here on the porch until you've done it."

"You'll take your foot out of my door?"

"Absolutely. The only reason I didn't let you close the

door was so you'd give me a second to explain myself. Trust me. If I'd wanted to gain entry to your house, this door—open or closed—would not stop me."

That she did not doubt for a second.

"Okay. I'll make the call."

To her surprise, his foot retracted and the door shut abruptly, making her stumble against it. Despite his assurance that he could force his way past it, she locked the dead bolt. It just made her feel better and maybe it would slow him down a little.

She picked up her cell phone and dialed the campus police. "Hi, this is Lily James. I'm the lady the three men attacked this afternoon."

"Ah, yes. Dr. James. How can I help you? Did you remember something that might help us catch your assailants?"

"Actually, I was wondering if you could tell me who the attacker was that jumped on me. The one you arrested."

"He was not one of your attackers, ma'am. It turns out he was a passerby. Army man with a combat background. He saw those men coming for you and tried to knock you out of the way."

"And you know for sure he's with the army?"

"Yes, ma'am. We spoke with his superiors. He's a decorated veteran with a sterling record. Apparently, he's on campus to speak with someone about something classified. His supervisors couldn't give us the details of that. But they assured us in the strongest possible terms that he's a man of absolute honor and trustworthiness."

"And you believed them?"

"Yes, ma'am. Do you know of some reason we shouldn't?"

"No," she replied thoughtfully. "Thanks."

"Call us if you remember any details about the other two men. Kidnapping is a serious crime."

No kidding. Especially when she was the target of it.

Lily hung up and made her way slowly back to the front door. So, he was who he said he was. She called through the panel. "Okay, I believe you. You're some army guy and you tried to save me today. Now what?"

She took a hasty step back as he answered from directly on the other side of the door. "How about you and I meet in a public place to talk, ma'am? Where you'll be surrounded by witnesses and perfectly safe. I won't be able to go into the details of what we need to discuss, but you can decide for yourself if I'm a bad guy or not."

"What kind of public place?" she asked, surprised by the suggestion. She'd assumed he would insist on coming into her living room right now. She was relieved that he wasn't going to invade her private sanctuary.

"Let's meet any place you'd be comfortable. How about a restaurant? I haven't eaten since this morning. Are you hungry, ma'am? We could have dinner together."

"Stop calling me ma'am. It makes me feel like my great-aunt Mildred."

"All right, ma'— Dr. James. How about it? You name the restaurant. I'll leave now and meet you there in, say, a half hour. My treat—so pick the most expensive joint in town. Preferably some place that serves a big slab of steak."

"Meat in large quantities isn't good for your digestion. Humans are chemically designed to be vegetarians, or at worst, occasional omnivores."

A sigh drifted through the door. "I'll eat alfalfa sprouts and dandelions if you'll just talk to me. Please?"

"All right. Fine. There's a place on Third Street, the Campus Club. It serves both meat and non-meat dishes, and they serve late. I'll meet you there in a half hour."

"Perfect." He sounded genuinely relieved. "I'm going to head for my car now. Watch me through the front window until I've driven away and you know I'm gone. I'll head over to this club of yours and get us a table. I'll be waiting for you. Don't be late."

His admonition to be punctual bugged her. She never had been any good at taking orders. She popped off, "What'll you do if I am late? Arrest me?"

He answered evenly, "I'd hate to have to resort to that, but yes, I suppose that would be my next step."

Seriously? She stood there, stunned, as his footsteps retreated across her porch and down her front steps. Arrest her? Could he do that? Who on earth was this guy?

Belatedly, she moved to her front window to stare at his retreating silhouette. He had broad, muscular shoulders or maybe it was just that his waist was lean and hard that made them look so big. He carried himself with an easy grace that made her feel gawky and uncoordinated just watching him.

He got into a nondescript sedan that screamed rental car. The headlights came on, the vehicle pulled away from the curb and its red taillights retreated down the street. As soon as they disappeared, she raced to her bathroom and threw on the light. Her hair was a disaster and she didn't have on a stitch of makeup. She ran a brush through the tangled chocolate mass and reached for a tube of mascara before it dawned on her what she was doing. What idiot primped for some guy who'd tackled her and scared her to death?

She threw the mascara into a drawer and stomped out of the bathroom. When she reached her closet, she pulled out holey jeans and the rattiest T-shirt she owned, a paint-stained thing that had seen much better days. She slammed her feet into sandals, grabbed her car keys, and headed for her garage. Cautiously, she backed out. Carter Baigneaux might not have tried to kidnap her, but someone else definitely had. Even Carter said so.

She guided the car down the street, watching her rearview mirror nervously. By the time she reached the Campus Club, which was indeed one of the most expensive restaurants near the university, she was getting downright paranoid. Twice, she identified cars that were definitely following her only to have them turn off on side streets a few moments later.

She circled the block twice before a parking spot opened up practically at the restaurant's door. Perfect. She ducked into the spot and made a dash for it. As she stepped into the dark paneled, old-world decor of the Campus Club, she checked her watch and was smug to see that she was five minutes late. She never had been a conformist and she wasn't about to start now.

A maitre d' she recognized from previous visits stepped forward. "Dr. James? Your party is waiting for you. This way."

The table he led her to, a white linen-covered affair set with crystal and china, made her feel violently under-dressed. Carter stood up to his full, imposing height as she approached. Something girly within her wished she'd dressed up for him before the defiant streak in her guffawed at the concept. Darned if he didn't step forward and pull out her chair for her. Startled, she sank into the seat as he pushed it in. Polite guy. He made her feel downright churlish for having intentionally dressed sloppily.

"Do you always hold chairs for women, or are you trying to butter me up?"

He shrugged. "I'm a Southern boy and I was raised old-school. Gentlemen hold chairs for ladies. My daddy still holds my mother's chair for her every night when they sit down to dinner, and they've been married going on forty years."

Okay, now she definitely felt bad. "I'm sorry I didn't have time to clean up more," she murmured.

"You look lovely just the way you are."

She felt herself reddening. A Southern boy, indeed. Quite the charmer. And speaking of which, she did detect a soft drawl beneath his matter-of-fact words. She asked, "Where in the South are you from, Captain?"

He grinned, flashing a killer smile that all but knocked her off her chair. "With a name like Baigneaux? I'm from Louisiana. Baton Rouge to be exact."

Flustered, she made a production of spreading her napkin in her lap.

"So tell me, Dr. James, do you have any idea who those men in the van were this afternoon?" he asked quietly.

She looked up quickly. "You don't know?" She'd assumed he knew who was after her because he was the one who presumably saved her from them.

"I have no idea whatsoever." He sounded grim enough to be telling the truth. "You?"

"No clue."

"Do you have any enemies? Has anyone threatened you recently?" he fired at her.

"I went over all of that with the campus police. No, I've received no threats, and other than the occasional whiny student who protests a bad grade, I have no enemies I'm aware of, Captain."

"How's your research going, Dr. James?"

The sharp change of topic from him threw her off balance.

"I've been having trouble with my computer model. The forecast physical- and radiation-damage patterns of superfast intergalactic flying objects aren't syncing up with my equations on stationary impacts."

"In English, please?" he murmured.

Oh. Right. Not a fellow astrophysicist. "I'm stuck on creating software to accurately predict what will happen when meteors hit the earth."

He leaned forwardly intently. "How stuck?"

She frowned. "Hard to tell. I haven't been able to get access to a big-enough computer to run a full simulation and calibrate my calculations. Bill Kaplan—he's the astronomy department chair—thinks I'm a crackpot and won't fund my work. So, until I can convince someone to cough up grant money for me, I'm pretty much dead in the water."

"What if I could help with that?"

She stared at the man across from her. "Are you serious?"

"As a heart attack, ma'— Dr. James."

"My first name's Lily. If you keep calling me Dr. James, I'm going to start feeling like I'm dating one of my students—" She broke off, appalled. "Not that this is a date—" She broke off again. "Or that you're remotely like one of my students—" She swore at herself silently. Sometimes she had the social skills of an amoeba.

A grin flickered around the edges of the captain's rather lovely mouth.

"Tell you what," he said easily. "I won't call you Doctor if you won't call me Captain. My first name's Carter. If you don't like that, my field handle's Boudreau or just Boo."

Boo? The moniker made him sound like a Pekingese. "Aren't you a little, uh, old for a name like Boo?"

He rolled his eyes. "Believe me, I had nothing to do with choosing it."

"Who gave it to you, then?"

"My teammates on Alpha Squa—" He broke off abruptly. "Some buddies of mine."

"What's a field handle?" she asked curiously.

He sighed. "A field handle is a nickname soldiers use in the field. It's usually shorter or easier to pronounce than a full last name."

She nodded. "Got it."

The waiter interrupted to take their orders. In spite of her earlier warning about its ill effects on his digestion, he ordered a prime rib with all the trimmings. She ordered a vegetarian ragout over soba. She was going to feel much better in a few hours than he was. Not to mention she was going to live decades longer than he would if he insisted on abusing his body like that.

They'd been engaged in casual dinner conversation for several minutes before it dawned on her that he'd put her entirely at ease with his rambling pleasantries. Smooth operator this man was. Although it probably didn't hurt his success factor that she was a complete dork around men in general and an easy mark for some charming Southerner to sweep off her feet.

There will be no feet-sweeping offage here, thank you very much. She told herself sternly not to be sucked in by this guy's Rhett Butler act.

After a thoroughly delicious meal, a waiter cleared their plates and poured coffee for them. Carter leaned forward, abruptly serious, his sapphire gaze intent. "So, tell me, Lily, has anyone shown an interest in your research recently?"

"Besides you?" she retorted. His gaze didn't waver an iota. She sighed. "Not that I'm aware of. But then, my preliminary equations are posted on the internet. Anyone could look at them and I'd never know."

"Could just anyone understand them?"

She answered candidly. "Probably not. It would take

a mathematician or physicist with a background in chaos theory to fully grasp the algorithms, I expect."

He smiled ruefully. "You make my head hurt with all those big words."

Her gaze narrowed. She wasn't fooled for a second. The man sitting across from her was highly intelligent. He might not be an astrophysicist, but he was sharp. She leaned forward herself. "Quit beating around the bush, Carter. What do you want from me?"

Their gazes locked. She was tempted to look away, but dealing with Bill Kaplan and the other self-righteous blowhards in the astronomy department who'd dismissed her for years as a nut job had made her tough. She might be hanging on to her position at the university by a thread, but by golly, she was still here.

"Suffice it to say that I would like to understand the full implications of your work. I think your research may be crucial to something I'm working on."

"And what might that be?" she asked, curious in spite of herself.

"I'm sorry. This isn't a secure location. I can't talk about it here. Is there any way you can come with me for a few days to discuss your work in more detail?"

Go with him? For *days?* Something fluttered deep in her belly. Something feminine and thrilled and, darn it, eager to say yes. "Can't…students…have to teach…lose my shot at tenure…" she stuttered, her tongue in a knot.

Carter waved a casual hand. "I can take care of that. I'll speak with your boss in the morning. He'll get someone to cover for you."

Bill Kaplan? Cover for her? No way. He would leap all over the excuse to fire her. The jerk had a new girl toy—an astronomy grad student whose only superfast intergalactic objects were her 38 double-Ds zooming around the campus observatory trying to look busy—and Kaplan had made it clear he wanted Lily's staff position for Astronomer Barbie.

She shook her head and said firmly, "I'm sorry. It's impossible. I absolutely cannot take any time off until the end of the semester. I can't risk losing my position here."

Carter merely grinned. "Impossible's my specialty."

Now why did that send a frisson of delight skittering up her spine?

He was speaking again. "…know where I can find your boss tomorrow morning?"

"He has office hours from nine to eleven—" She broke off. "But I'm serious. You can't talk to him. I really need this job. It's the only way I'll be able to get grant money and no one else will hire me until I can prove that I'm not crazy—" Darn it. She'd done it again. She'd gone and stuck her foot in her mouth like a proper dimwit. "I'm not crazy, mind you. I just have some theories that challenge conventional wisdom…"

She trailed off. Carter was smiling broadly at her. "If I thought you were crazy, I wouldn't be sitting here talking with you. I think you're onto something and I need your help."

He thought she was onto something? Really? Whether it was mere relief or desperate need for approval bubbling up inside her, the frothy happiness in her stomach was nice for a change. And it had *nothing* to do with what his smile did to her blood pressure.

True to his promise, Carter paid for dinner and escorted her to the door of the restaurant. She was surprised when he stopped in the vestibule, though. He murmured, "Would you like me to walk you to your car? Or should I wait here until you've driven away?"

She frowned. "Why do you ask?"

"I was probing delicately to find out if you're still worried that I'll kidnap you. I was trying to be sensitive."

"Oh. Sensitive. Right. Um, I guess I'm not afraid of you. But you don't need to walk me to my car. It's right out front."

He smiled painfully. "After that less-than-ringing endorsement, I'll definitely wait here until you're gone."

"Whatever floats your boat, Rhett."

"Excuse me?"

"Oh, uh, nothing," she mumbled, chagrined. Good grief. She was so lame. Mortified, she reached for the door, but then it opened magically before her. A powerful arm had shot out from behind her and pushed it out of the way. She glanced up into Carter's wry gaze. He was standing so close that she felt the heat radiating from his body. Her pulse galloped wildly all of a sudden.

"What can I say?" he murmured. "I'm old-school."

Rhett Butler, indeed. She stepped into the chilly evening air, her cheeks hotter than they ought to be. True to his word, Carter didn't follow her outside. Regret speared through her. Why hadn't she simpered and cooed and vowed she needed a big strong man to protect her across all twelve feet of sidewalk to her li'l ol' car?

She scowled at her car and reached for the door handle. And that was when the twin, fast-moving shadows rushed her out of nowhere. Strong arms wrapped around her, and someone slapped something wet and cold over her mouth and nose. She fought for her life, flailing and trying to shout for help as best she could around the choking fumes filling her nostrils. But it was no use. Her assailants were bigger and stronger than her by a lot.

Her last, vague thought as her legs collapsed out from under her was that maybe she should've played helpless after all and manipulated Carter into walking her to her car.

* * *

Carter had worked with enough women in his day who could handle themselves in a pinch to know without a doubt that Lily James was *not* one of them. The woman was scary smart, but a little short on common sense if he didn't miss his guess. Still, when she'd looked up at him with those big, impossibly soft brown eyes of hers and passed by close enough for him to smell sunshine and honey on her skin, his pulse leaped. The girl had a way of getting under a guy's skin.

He gave her a short head start before he stepped out into the night behind her. No sense scaring her again after he'd just spent most of the evening calming her down. He'd barely taken a step outside before he saw them. Two men struggling with a slender form between them, this time without crowds of bystanders to force them to flee.

He reached for his gun. Ice picks of pain shot down his arm and the big muscles of his back clenched spasmodically. The silenced pistol slid easily out of its oiled holster, fitting into his palm like an old friend. He started to shout a warning when a tourniquet of agony wrapped around his throat without warning. His thighs locked up and then his calves wrenched into masses of cramps that all but brought him to his knees. He swore violently as his mind tried to become a block of ice.

At least his weapon was in the clear. Desperately, he clenched his finger around the trigger. He managed to raise his arm. Squeeze the trigger. The pistol kicked, making a low spit of sound.

One of the men cried out and let go of Lily. Carter aimed clumsily at the broad back of the second man. Lily was in trouble. She needed him. He was her only hope of rescue in the next few, critical seconds. *Squeeze. The. Trigger.*

He gritted his teeth and fired. The weapon jumped in

his hand. The second man shouted something and Carter mentally lurched. He recognized that language. The curse was uttered in *Russian!* What the heck?

He tried with all his might to drag his right leg forward. Intense pain coursed through him, but his shoe skidded a few inches across the pavement. *Must. Save. Lily.* Now his left leg.

The first man was climbing to his feet, nursing his right arm. Moving like Frankenstein's monster, Carter bent his torso stiffly from the hips, bringing his right hand and the pistol clutched in it to bear on the assailant.

The man babbled something in Russian. It took Carter's pain-riddled brain a second to realize the guy was begging for his life. Good thing he was the guy with the gun. Otherwise this encounter would be going very differently. But then Carter spied Lily crumpled on the curb like a rag doll behind the guy and all sympathy for the Russian drained out of him. Cold death in his gaze, he glared back at the injured assailant.

His deadly intent must have been clear because, as Carter raised the pistol one more time, the guy darted to his comrade, dragging the more seriously wounded man's arm across his shoulder. The two men retreated down the street too quickly for Carter to chase after them. He had no authorization to kill on this mission, and besides, Lily needed help.

Lily. He turned and fell to his knees beside her.

"Lil. Lee," he managed to grunt hoarsely.

He heard tires squeal in the distance. The Russians' van must have been waiting nearby. But all his concern was for the woman on the ground before him. She looked so small and helpless. He felt like his guts were being ripped out of him by slow degrees.

"Lil. Lee."

Nothing. Frantically, he watched her rib cage. It rose and fell, and he sagged with relief. He wasn't strong enough yet to lift her. The freeze-up lifted gradually and he had no choice but to wait it out.

What kind of man couldn't pick up a woman who'd fainted and carry her to safety? A worthless shell of a man who was so screwed up in the head that he had full-body seizures every time he got even the slightest bit stressed out.

His throat muscles began to relax. He crooned words of comfort to her as the small muscles in his body started to unwind. He wiggled his fingers and toes, willing his major muscle groups to hurry up and regain full functionality. Finally, *finally,* he was able to reach out and smooth the silky strands of her hair off her porcelain cheeks.

"Wake up, sugar. C'mon. Wake up for me," he murmured. Dammit. They must have drugged her. This was no faint. She was out cold. He had to get her out of here before those Russians patched up their injuries and decided to come back and finish the job. Clearly, they had some sort of powerful motivation to kidnap Lily. Why else would they have attempted to snatch her for a second time in a single day? Were they on as tight a timetable as he was?

A sinking feeling filled his stomach. If they were in such an all-fire hurry, how could they not be after her for the very same reason he was? He swore under his breath. He had to get her out of here. Away from the Russians.

Carter wasn't sure yet if he could trust his muscles, but it wasn't like he had any choice. He bent down awkwardly, scooped her up in his arms and staggered down the street to his car. He had barely enough coordination to dump her in the passenger seat and strap in her inert form, but he managed both.

He surely didn't have enough coordination to drive yet,

but that was just his tough luck. The worst of it was getting the car keys out of his pocket and into the ignition. He had to get away from here before the Russians called in reinforcements and came back to finish the job. If he could just get Lily out of town. Then he could stop and wait for her to wake up and for his body to fully unwind.

Thankfully, the hour was late and the streets mostly deserted. Driving like his grandmother, he avoided major highways and headed out of town. He guided the vehicle east into the deserted wastes of the California desert.

He had a serious problem on his hands. What if the Russian government had stumbled across Lily's research paper on the internet the same way he had? And what if they'd extrapolated the same possibility? Surely, they'd be hell-bent to get their hands on her to silence her and hide the predictions her algorithms made.

No matter how he sliced it, the answer kept coming out exactly the same. The Russians would have to do something drastic to stop her from talking to anyone who would understand the full implications of her work. They *had* to imprison her—or possibly even kill her.

Chapter 2

Lily woke up slowly. Her neck hurt, and she was seated in an oddly uncomfortable position. She registered silence around her along with a faint glow of green light. Her eyelids fluttered open.

"Welcome back, sugar," a male voice murmured beside her.

She jolted in alarm, coming fully awake in a rush of panic. She stared at the man in the driver's seat. Oh. Carter. She relaxed. "Where are we? What hap—" She broke off, trying to sort the jumble of images returning to her. "You held the door for me…and I went to my car…and then… Oh!"

"Yeah," Carter commented drily. "Oh."

"Who were those men?"

"Russians as far as I can tell."

She stared at him in disbelief. "Why on earth would some Russian guys try to kidnap me? And where are we?"

He chose to answer her second question first. "We're in eastern California. I need to get you to a military base ASAP. As for your first question, I suspect it has to do with your research."

"I lob hypothetical rocks at a simulated Earth. What's the big deal about that? And since when is there a military base in this area?"

Was he implying there was a classified base out here? Like the real Area 51 maybe? The side of her that secretly, desperately hoped to meet an alien in her lifetime silently whooped in excitement.

He didn't answer either question, merely started the car and turned on the air conditioner.

She asked the next most obvious question. "If we're in such a hurry to get to this secret military base that I'm not supposed to know exists, why are we sitting at the side of a road going nowhere?"

"I, uh, have a little problem."

She looked up sharply. Even in the faint glow of the dashboard, she made out humiliation suffusing his face. "What's wrong?"

"I was in a…situation…a while back. Saw some things. Did some things…" He broke off for a long moment before continuing heavily, "Ever since, I have these, um, episodes."

Alarm coursed through her. In his episodes, did he go psychotic and kill helpless female astrophysicists perchance? "What kind of episodes?" she asked carefully.

"Both the neurologists and the shrinks say the seizures are psychological. I just freeze up. Can't move. I got us out of town, but I thought it might be wise to let my body come back to fully functional before I drive any further."

"Oh, thank goodness," she said in relief.

"Excuse me?" Disbelief laced his voice. Maybe even a touch of outrage crept into it.

She waved a breezy hand. "I was worried that it was something really bad."

"This is really bad!" he blurted a shade indignantly.

She shrugged. "So, your body checks out now and then. It's not like you black out and turn into an ax murderer."

"When you put it that way, I'm doing just spiffy," he retorted, his voice thick with sarcasm.

"I'm serious," she replied. "It could be a lot worse."

"Your middle name isn't Pollyanna by any chance, is it?"

She rolled her eyes. "I'm just saying. We all have our crosses to bear. You could be dying."

He shook his head at her. "You have no idea. I can't do my job—" He broke off.

She said with a trace of reproach, "Stephen Hawking is one of the greatest scientists ever to live, and he can't even talk. He has to type with a visual interface device, one painstaking letter at a time, to communicate some of the most brilliant thinking ever recorded. How frustrating must it be to have all that genius trapped inside a body that can *never* move?"

Carter looked taken aback. "All right already. My life is fabulous by comparison."

She subsided, studying him closely. "How long do these episodes usually last?"

"They've been getting shorter. I'm down to somewhere between two and ten minutes. Although—" he frowned "—this one's been going for an inordinately long time."

"How long did they used to be?"

"The first one lasted two weeks. That was right after the ambu—er, situation."

"Ambush? Were you attacked?" Consternation at the

thought of this nice man being in danger coursed through her. "Was everyone okay?"

He answered quietly, "No. Everyone was not okay. That's why the shrinks think I'm like this. They think my mind is punishing me or something. Whenever someone's life depends on me now, I freeze up."

She looked outside the car in quick alarm. Her life depended on him in some way? Was there some immediate threat she wasn't aware of? "Who's threatening my life right now?"

"No one this second. I'm still unwinding from that attack back at the restaurant."

Her breathing accelerated. "Exactly how much danger *am* I in?"

He closed his eyes and squeezed them shut for several long seconds before he answered her soothingly, "I'm trained to think in worst-case scenarios. To anticipate bad stuff so I can stop it before it happens. I'm sure you'll be fine."

He hadn't answered her question. And whatever worst case awaited her, it was bad enough to keep him a statue for a good long time. "What can I do to help you with this condition of yours?" she asked.

"Nothing."

She leaned across the seats to place a hand on his shoulder. "Have you tried massage to relax your muscles?"

"Trust me. We've tried everything," he ground out.

But as her hand rested lightly on his shoulder, she thought she felt the rigid muscle softening slightly beneath her fingers. She kneaded a little, experimentally. That was a definite easing of the terrible tension under her palm.

"Did you feel that?" she asked.

"Yes. I did." He sounded startled. "Do that again."

Unbuckling her seat belt, she maneuvered until she was

kneeling in her seat and resting her hands on each of his shoulders. It brought her into intimately close proximity with him, but he didn't voice any complaints or make any inappropriate comments. Must be that old-school gentleman thing kicking in.

She massaged his shoulders, and in moments, the muscles noticeably relaxed. She bent to the task with more enthusiasm. "I need more room to reach the rest of you," she announced.

"Electric seat. Push the switch by my left hip." He sounded more than a little uncomfortable.

Lily reached across his lap and found the switch. His seat was already most of the way back because he was a big man, but she motored it back the last few inches and reclined it as well. She swung her right leg across his lap and straddled his thighs.

"Better," she stated.

He looked equal parts amused and frustrated. "Damn," he muttered. "A pretty girl climbs on top of me and I'm supposed to just lie here and look at her."

She frowned, intent on her experiment. "Let's see if we can fix that." She commenced working in earnest on his neck and shoulders, moving on to his chest as his muscles became supple and relaxed under her massaging fingers.

When he groaned quietly, her hands froze, but the sound was pure pleasure.

Good gravy, the man felt amazing. He was slabbed in muscle everywhere she touched. Greek statues came to mind as she tried to envision what her fingers were outlining.

She reached behind herself to massage his thighs near his knees, but it wasn't enough to relax his legs entirely. She rose to her knees and reached for his hips, digging her fingers deep into his flanks. He groaned wordlessly, and she almost did the same. Her hands slid across the tops of his thighs, and abruptly she became aware that she was all but massaging the man's crotch. Her hands had unconsciously strayed in the same directions her thoughts were heading.

"Uh, sorry," she mumbled.

He laughed under his breath. "No apologies whatsoever are necessary. You're a miracle worker."

The fervent pleasure in his voice made her cheeks warm in embarrassment. She was such a hussy, climbing all over this poor man when he was defenseless. Seriously. Here she was getting all turned on, and he was sitting there, possibly in terrible pain.

"Am I hurting you?" she blurted.

"Not in the way you mean," he ground out between what sounded like clenched teeth.

"Huh?"

"Never mind, sugar." His eyes blazed at her and her entire body blazed back.

And then the side of her hand bumped against a muscle that was definitely not paralyzed and jumped hard at her accidental touch. *Oh.* He was in *that* kind of pain. Her cheeks exploded into fire.

"Have I missed anywhere?" Sheesh. She sounded all out of breath like she'd been running…or was so hot-to-trot she couldn't breathe right.

He startled her by raising his hands clumsily to the small of her back. "Sugar, that felt better than just about anything I can ever remember. Any chance I could hire you to be my personal masseuse for the rest of my life?"

She stared down at him, her jaw sagging. Personal masseuse? Rest of his life? Her brain hitched and actually stopped processing information momentarily. She finally managed to mumble, "Really? That felt good?"

Carter shifted beneath her, and abruptly she realized she wasn't straddling a statue anymore. He was a living, breathing, fully mobile and functional male. A big, strong one. And she was sitting in his very aroused lap.

He stared back at her. "You do know how attractive a woman you are, don't you?"

The abrupt shift of topic gave her mental whiplash. "Me? Well, I…attractive?" she managed to squeak.

"Oh, for the love God. You don't, do you?" His arms swept around her upper torso and pulled her down to him too quickly for her to do anything but yield to the pressure. She fell forward, shamelessly savoring the way his chest mashed hers and made her think distinctly unprofessorly thoughts.

His mouth closed on hers and established immediately that neither his lips nor his tongue were the slightest bit affected by psychosomatic paralysis. His mouth was warm and resilient against hers as his hand on the back of her neck tugged her down to him more firmly.

"You taste like peach pie," he murmured against her mouth, "and ice cream." His tongue dipped between her lips to sample more of her. "Drizzled with honey. On a warm summer day."

As for what he tasted like, if heaven had a taste, this was it. She moaned aloud as she writhed against his chest and her entire body sang with pleasure. Heck, her body was belting out an entire hallelujah chorus of pleasure. But then, way down deep within her core, a part of her went still and silent. Waiting. Wanting. Yearning.

"I think I want you," Lily murmured in amazement.

"You don't have to sound so stunned." He laughed against her mouth. "You'll give me a worse complex than I already have about my manhood."

"I'm stunned at me, not you," she retorted. "And what's

wrong with your manhood? You're a god. Of course any woman would find you wildly attractive."

"You've got that wrong, darlin'. I'm no god. I'm damned to eternal hell. I figure this little problem of mine is just a foretaste of things to come." He pulled her closer then, wrapping her in his gentle but inexorable strength.

And she drank up every bit of it, relishing the dangerous taste of him on her tongue. "Make love to me," she gasped, reaching for his belt buckle.

His hands closed over hers. "Not now. Not like this. If I make love to you, I'll be at full strength, not half-frozen and unable to do you justice. And it certainly won't be in a car. I gave up on that long before I got out of high school. I like my women and my lovemaking surfaces to be civilized."

"That's not what you said before."

He laughed. "I never said what I like to *do* with either of them is remotely civilized, darlin'."

A shiver of delight raced down her spine. Her mind stumbled and then thrilled at the thought of what more awaited her in this man's arms. And he'd said "*when* I make love to you," not if. A revealing slip of the tongue that.

He nibbled her neck just enough to send spears of lust shooting down her torso to parts of her that needed no further encouragement to burn. "As much as I'd love to take you out under the stars and make love to you, sugar, we've got to go. You're still in danger."

"Are you fit to drive?" she whispered against his collarbone. She kissed her way across the bulge of his shoulder muscle and then back to his neck.

He laughed shortly. "If you don't stop that I won't be fit to drive. But it won't be a seizure disabling me, woman."

She drew back, staring at him in open disbelief. She had the power to arouse a man like him? Her? But she was scrawny and bookish and always forgot to do something with her hair or put on any makeup. She spent her nights staring at the sky and her days doing complex mathematical calculations. She wasn't exactly sexpot material. But the physical evidence of his attraction to her was impossible to miss. Impossible to argue with.

For a reasonably intelligent woman, her brain was taking an inordinately long time wrapping itself around this new concept of being sexy to someone. But she liked the idea. A lot. More than a lot.

It dawned on her that she wanted to drive this man out of his mind sexually possibly worse than anything else she'd ever wanted. And she'd wanted to get her Ph.D. and study the universe pretty darn badly. It had been her defining force in life for the past twenty years or more.

"Once I'm safely inside your precious military base, is there a chance we might continue this?" she asked in a breathless voice she hardly recognized as her own.

He grinned at her and replied, his Louisiana drawl suddenly thick, "Oh, there's a chance all right. My mama didn't raise no dummy. I know better than to walk away from your kind of fire, *chère*."

Chapter 3

What on *earth* had that woman done to him? Never, ever, had any therapy from the scores of doctors who'd worked on him even come close to Lily's hands for effectiveness. All she had to do was touch him and he melted beneath her fingers like magic. She must be an angel sent to deliver him from his private hell. He hadn't the faintest idea what he'd done to deserve her, but he knew one thing. He was intensely grateful for the gift of her.

He drove in silence through the night. She glanced over at him occasionally, a sidelong, flirty little look, and every time she did, the temperature in the car went up by several degrees. Who'd have guessed a brilliant astrophysicist could be so sexy that it took every bit of his military discipline to keep his hands off her?

She was a little thing, and it was easy to miss the perfection of her curves underneath those nondescript clothes. But in a way, they added to the appeal. It was as if she was his own personal secret, his to unwrap and discover before anyone else did.

Desperate to distract himself from fantasies that threatened to send the car into a ditch as he lost himself in them, he eventually asked, "What's that bright star straight ahead? The one hanging low on the horizon?"

"That's not a star. It's Saturn. Next time we're at my place, I'll pull out my telescope and let you have a look at her rings. They're beautiful. Or even better, come with me to the university's observatory and I'll give you a look at her you'll never forget."

Damn if it wasn't sexy listening to her talk about some planet. He asked hastily, "How did you get interested in astrophysics?"

"*Star Trek* reruns."

"Original or Next Generation?" he asked, amused.

She considered the question as if world peace hung in the balance, eventually answering thoughtfully, "There's no denying Captain Picard was a hottie. But there's something about Captain Kirk's brand of macho that a girl has to love."

He broke into a grin as she continued earnestly, "I kept asking my elementary-school teachers if any of the science on the show was real, and they couldn't tell me. So I started investigating it for myself. Turns out there are wormholes after all. And some of the dimensional theory on the show was actually pretty close to what we now believe to be true."

He grinned at her. "I'd be happy if I could just teleport."

"I'd be thrilled if we could just travel at faster than light speed," she shot back.

"Why?"

"Because then we'd actually stand a chance of reaching other planets that sustain intelligent life."

"Are scientists getting close to high-speed space travel?" he asked curiously.

"I wish. We may be approaching the theory of it, but I fear it'll be a long time before we can translate theory into practical use."

He shrugged. "Ah, well. I like good ol' Earth well enough."

Carter happened to glance over at her in time to catch a shadow crossing her expressive features. "What were you thinking just then?" he asked quietly.

She looked up at him, her gaze sober. "I was thinking about how long I've wished I could get off this planet."

Alarm coursed through him. She wasn't suicidal, was she? He blurted quickly, "But if you left, I couldn't collect on your promise to continue where we left off before."

Her eyes widened. "I thought you were the one who promised me."

"A promise like that goes both ways, *chère*."

And just like that, the air was thick and heavy and pulsing with sexual promise between them. At least the stress of being so in lust with her that he could barely see straight wasn't sending him into marble statue mode. Only one part of him was rock solid at the moment.

He was too turned on to get sleepy and she'd just had a chloroform-induced nap, so they both were wide awake when he turned onto a narrow, dirt road at nearly 4:00 a.m.

"Are we getting close?" she asked eagerly.

"Yup. By the way, you're going to have to sign a bunch of paperwork promising not to reveal the existence of this place or else the government really will have to shoot you."

"Cool," she murmured.

Her enthusiasm was contagious. Smiling to himself, he turned down another unmarked road. A few minutes later, a small shack came into sight tucked under a rock overhang. He turned off his headlights and approached the structure with only his parking lights illuminated. He stopped beside the shack and rolled down his window.

An armed guard wearing body armor stepped up to the car.

"I'm Captain Carter Baigneaux. I believe y'all are expecting me?"

"Yes, sir. H.O.T. Watch called and said you needed some emergency assistance. We've got a cabin waiting for you and your guest. I'll need to see picture identification for both of you."

Carter passed the guy his military ID and Lily handed over her driver's license. The guard disappeared inside the building for a moment. When he returned, he handed back their IDs and leaned down to say through the window, "Welcome to Camp Nowhere, Dr. James."

"Thank you," she murmured, eagerness all but rolling off her. She was practically bouncing in her seat. Sometimes he forgot that the secret world he lived in had cool factor to outsiders. To him, it was just his job.

Carter eased the car forward into what looked like more of the same desert they'd been driving through. He said to her, "There aren't alien spaceships or carcasses stashed out here, you know."

"What is this place, then?"

"I'm sorry, I can't tell you what they do here. It's just a place where we can get some sleep and have a secure space to talk about your work."

He turned the car where the guard had told him to and followed a one-lane dirt track up a hill into a stand of mesquite trees and desert willows. Nestled among them was a small wood-sided cabin. A covered porch extended across its front and a light shone in a window.

He got out of the car, feeling the worse for wear. The seizures took a toll on his body, and he ached from head to foot. "Sorry we weren't able to swing by your place and get any stuff for you. I'll see what the guys can scare up for you around here tomorrow."

"I'm just glad to be alive, Carter. I can survive without my toothbrush for a night. And it's not like I tend to primp much."

"You're lucky. You don't have to primp to be pretty."

"I bet you say that to all the girls."

He snorted. Aloud he explained, "In the first place, a gentleman never talks about his previous lady friends. And in the second place, you'd be surprised how scary some women look the morning after when the makeup's all gone and the hair's a mess. I'm speaking purely hypothetically, of course."

She laughed back. "Of course."

He climbed the steps and pushed open the front door. The cabin's interior was as rustic as its exterior, with wood-plank floors and walls, a stone fireplace, rough log furniture and even a pair of antlers hanging over the mantel.

"This is charming," Lily commented brightly.

He smiled his gratitude at her that she wasn't going to get picky over the simple accommodations. Somebody was probably having to sleep in his office tonight so they could use this place.

They took a quick tour of the cabin. There was only one bedroom, but the living-room sofa pulled out into a bed. He announced, "I'll take the sofa."

"You'll do no such thing," she stated firmly. "You've had a rough day and I weigh about half of what you do.

I'll be much more comfortable on the hide-a-bed than you'd be."

"I seem to recall you having a rather rough day yourself," he retorted. "Southern boy here, remember?"

She marched over and glared up at him. She made the world's cutest bantam hen with her feathers all ruffled up like this. "Don't make me have to beat you up," she threatened.

Carter laughed and surprised himself by sweeping her into a hug. For some reason, he couldn't seem to keep his hands off her. He murmured into her sweet-smelling hair, "Thanks again for helping me out before. But may I remind you we have no pajamas. If someone comes to check on us in the morning, wouldn't you rather have the privacy of the bedroom and let me answer the door in my boxers?"

"You're a boxer man, huh? I'd have pegged you for a briefs man."

He blinked, startled, and set her away from him. How had they gotten onto the subject of his underwear? He shook his head. "Take the bedroom. I'm used to sleeping in a lot worse places than this."

She opened her mouth to protest, but he really didn't feel like arguing anymore with her. So, he did the expedient thing and leaned down quickly to kiss her. As a distraction tactic went, it was spectacularly successful. It was a dirty trick to pull on her, but damned if he wasn't dying to have the excuse to kiss her again.

She made a surprised little sound in the back of her throat, and then she melted into him like butter on a hot cob of corn. He absorbed her into himself, amazed at how right she felt in his arms. His own personal angel.

Maybe it was just that she was the first woman he'd been close to like this since the ambush. He'd spent the past few months going from doctor to doctor while they tried to figure out what was wrong with him. Apparently, his paralysis thing wasn't a normal reaction to a mission gone bad. But then, it hadn't been a normal mission. It wasn't often a man was forced to kill children. They might have been violent, psychotic children raised from the age of four or five to be vicious killers, but apparently, it still did a number on a guy's head to mow down boys as young as ten. Even if they were pointing Uzis at him and his teammates with absolute intent to do murder.

Although that wasn't the bit that had messed with his head the worst. As long as he lived, he would never forget the village they'd come across where the child army had already done its worst. The streets had been littered with the mutilated bodies of girls and women, raped and hacked apart in the most brutal possible manner. How could *children* do that to women who could have been their own mothers and sisters?

He broke off the gruesome trip down memory lane and realized with a start that Lily had gone still in his arms. "What's wrong?" he murmured.

"You tell me. One second you were here with me, and the next you'd checked out. You're not having another episode, are you?"

"I certainly hope not," he replied grimly. "Sorry. Mind strayed there."

She wilted in his arms. It was his turn to ask in quick alarm, "What's wrong?"

"I was hoping that kissing me would hold your attention better than that."

He laughed aloud. "Lily, you're so attractive I'm having to fight like crazy to think about anything but dragging you into that bedroom and making love to you right this second."

She blinked up at him owlishly. "Really?"

He muttered more to himself than her, "Crazy astrophysicist. The woman casually does calculus that would make a grown man cry but can't even see herself clearly in the mirror. You're a beautiful, sexy, desirable woman, dammit."

Soft, small hands cupped his cheeks. "Until I can see myself that way, will you keep on telling me what you see?"

He gazed down at her seriously. "That's a deal. We've got a long day ahead of us tomorrow. Get some sleep, okay?"

"Such a gentleman," she murmured under her breath. She gave his cheek a pat before turning him loose and heading for the bedroom.

He grimaced at her retreating back. If she only knew the totally ungentlemanly thoughts he was having about what he'd like to do to her, she wouldn't be so quick to say that.

Lily couldn't sleep. Whether it was because she'd already had several hours of forced rest earlier, or because she couldn't figure out why some Russians could possibly want to kidnap her or because she was so hot and bothered over the man snoozing in the other room, she couldn't say. But she knew one thing for sure. She was not letting Carter Baigneaux slip away from her anytime soon.

Problem was, she didn't have any idea how to act like the sexy, desirable woman he seemed to think she was. She was a scientist. She formed theories and performed experiments to prove or disprove them. She sighed. Maybe she should just apply her scientific techniques to this situation, too. Her mind wandered idly.

Hypothesis: It was possible for her to land a sexy

hunk like Carter if she applied the right preparation and technique to the project.

Plan of attack: Ascertain what Carter liked in his women. Assuming it was even possible for her to be those things, transform herself into that kind of woman with all due haste. In the meantime, take every opportunity to be near him, particularly within kissing range.

Note to self: Do not appear desperate or pushy if at all possible. Just be available. Convenient.

List of required supplies: Makeup, hairbrush, toothbrush, perfume, sexy clothes. Even better, some sexy lingerie to be left draped on a bedpost or someplace he could see it. A short skirt maybe. She'd been told before she had great legs.

Okay. She could do this. If her hypothesis was valid, Carter Baigneaux would inevitably become hers. A plan of attack in place, she fell asleep debating sexy red lipstick or a soft and feminine shade of pink.

A few hours later she jolted awake to sunlight pouring in the window and the sound of a knock on her door. Carter announced through the panel, "Lily, we have a visitor. You might want to get dressed and come meet him."

Dang! She'd planned to sashay out into the living room in just her old T-shirt this morning and give Carter an eyeful of her rather nice legs. Disappointed, she rolled out of bed, yanked on her jeans and headed for the bathroom. She splashed water on her face, pulled her hair back into a utilitarian ponytail and regretfully put Operation Land Sexy Hunk on hold.

She stepped into the living room and was startled to see a gray-haired man in an olive-green uniform complete with—gulp—stars on his shoulders.

"Lily, this is General Fiske. Sir, this is Dr. Lily James, the astrophysicist H.O.T. Watch told you about."

Lily shook the hand the general offered her and managed not to wince at the man's painful grip.

"Nice to meet you, Doctor," he rumbled. "We've arranged a place for you to work while you're with us. I took the liberty of having some breakfast sent over there so you can get right to it. We're eager to hear what you can tell us about our crisis—"

Carter interrupted. "I haven't briefed her in yet, sir. Haven't been in a secure location to do it."

"Hmm. Well, then. Yes. Must get you two to work right away. Time is of the essence, Captain."

Carter nodded briskly at the general while Lily stared at him. A crisis? What crisis? He hadn't said anything about a crisis! Alarmed, she followed the men from the cabin. Carter helped her up into the backseat of a black Hummer, then climbed in beside her as the general took shotgun. A driver guided the vehicle down the narrow drive.

After checking what the driver could see in the rearview mirror, she eased her hand across the backseat to lay it on Carter's thigh. She craved the reassurance of his touch right now.

She was on a secret military installation, some crisis was brewing and they thought she had all the answers? She was just some nobody assistant professor whom her colleagues unanimously believed had a screw loose. How was she supposed to explain to Carter that he'd be wise not to depend on her for any help at all?

He seemed to sense her disquiet, for he laid his big, warm hand over hers and squeezed gently. Even better, he didn't draw his hand away or push hers off his leg. Although unmistakably powerful, his thigh muscles were relaxed beneath her palm this morning. No sign of a seizure or whatever it was that ailed him. As soon as she had a free moment and access to the internet, she planned to do a little research of her own on this condition of his. He didn't strike her as the kind of person to have random, full-body seizures without a darn good reason for them.

"Here we are," General Fiske announced. Lily jumped and yanked her hand out from under Carter's as the vehicle abruptly stopped.

She frowned. And where exactly was *here?* All she saw was another cabin, somewhat more ramshackle than theirs had been, nestled up against the side of a huge outcropping of red sandstone.

Perplexed, she followed the two men into the tiny building. And then all became clear. The cabin was merely a shell over what looked like basically a lobby. A stainless-steel elevator door loomed in front of them, and armed guards stood at attention on either side of it.

"At ease, men," the general said.

In unison, the guards took a single step to spread their boots shoulder-width apart and placed a hand behind their backs. If that was their idea of being at ease, she'd hate to see their idea of rigid and tense.

The elevator door whooshed open and she followed Carter and the general into the conveyance. Ugh. She genuinely disliked little boxes that whisked her up and down at breathtaking speeds. The elevator lurched slightly and descended fast. Her ears popped and she tried to guess how far underground they were but had no idea. Possibly many hundreds of feet.

After a full minute, the doors opened on a brightly lit white corridor that looked like it came straight out of a bad science-fiction movie. "Where are the people in the white lab coats carrying clipboards?" she murmured.

Carter's mouth twitched and his eyes sparkled at her but he didn't reply.

The general strode up to an unmarked door and threw

it open with a flourish. Curious, she stepped inside to see a small, square room decorated in more unimaginative— and blinding—white. White boards were mounted on two walls, and a gray metal desk sat against the third wall, a computer and printer on top of it. Two chairs sat in front of the desk.

"Top-of-the-line system there," General Fiske said proudly.

She glanced at it and frowned. She'd had a more powerful system than that in her office several years ago. But she held her tongue as Carter rolled his eyes at her behind the general's back.

"You two get to work and save the world now, you hear?" And with that, Fiske backed out of the room and closed the door behind him.

Lily rounded on Carter. "What's this about a crisis? We're supposed to save the world?"

He replied in a falsely bright voice, "All in good time. Why don't you crank up that dinosaur and see what it'll do?"

She frowned and sat down at the desk to boot up the computer. Her frown deepened when Carter commenced examining the walls and ceiling in minute detail. The system had woken up and she was entertaining herself adding layers of password encryption to the log-in sequence when Carter finally leaned down over her shoulder.

"No cameras. The room's clear," he murmured, his lips moving lightly against her ear.

Oh, my. Operation Hunk for Lunch was back in play. Big-time.

She half turned in her seat and was preparing to stand up and give the target of her experiment a proper good-morning hug, and maybe even a kiss, when the door opened behind Carter without warning.

He straightened casually and turned around. She peered out from behind him and saw a young man in fatigue pants and an olive-green T-shirt wheeling in a cart with steaming plates of food and a coffeepot on it.

"Thanks, Sergeant," Carter said. "And could you put a note on the door to have people knock before they come in?"

"Yes, sir. Right away." The sergeant backed out of the room.

"Ooh. I like it when you go all military and commanding like that," she purred.

Carter laughed. "Don't tempt me, sugar. We have work to do."

"Right. We're supposed to save the world. Did I mention that I'm a tiny bit claustrophobic? I don't know how long I'm going to be able to stand being down here."

He momentarily looked concerned, but then his eyes lit in a smile. "Let me know when you need distraction. I'm sure I can come up with a way to take your mind off being fifteen hundred feet underground. I've learned a thing or two from all the shrinks who worked on me for the past few months."

"Fifteen hundred—" her breathing accelerated rapidly. "I'm not kidding, Carter. I really hate confined spaces. And being buried alive like this ranks right up there on the freak-out scale."

He stepped close enough that she caught the scent of soap and shaving cream and her breath hitched. "I'm not kidding either. I can jam that door lock so no one can get in here anytime soon and we can do all the distracting you need."

"Explain to me again how wild monkey sex is going to save the world?" she mumbled.

He laughed. "Ah, you are enough to test a man's self-control." He smiled regretfully at her as he added, "And you're right. We really do have to get to work. Okay, here's the deal. You did a preliminary test run of your equations on an asteroid a while back. A-57809C."

She nodded. "It's an insignificant little chunk of rock due to hit Earth in a few weeks. It's big enough that it won't burn up in the atmosphere, but not so big anyone's worried about it. I was hoping to run my calculations on it and then get grant money to go to Siberia after it lands and measure exactly how accurate my predictions turn out to be. But I can't even get money to run the calculations, let alone go see if I'm right."

"If you could run the simulation, what sort of damage would you expect to see in the impact zone?"

"I can't be certain. That's what the equations are for."

"Come now. Surely you've plugged in some estimates and crunched them just to see what you'd get."

"Well, yes," she replied doubtfully. "But they're guesses at best."

"Indulge me. What do you *guess* your equations will suggest by way of damage?"

Guessing made the scientist in her intensely uncomfortable. But she nodded gamely and answered him. "Well, the asteroid's core appears to be iron. When it explodes on impact, it should throw out a decent-size electromagnetic pulse. If there were people in the area, their electricity, radio, television, computers—anything with a microchip in it—would be wiped out."

"Go on."

She continued, "The region should experience what feels like a small earthquake and any standing foliage immediately around the impact point could be flattened by the shock wave. The main impact crater should be about fifty feet or so across and about half that deep. If this rock were to hit a city, the death toll could run into the hundreds. But as it is, only a few Siberian hares should get cooked and maybe a few reindeer. It's going to hit a truly desolate region."

He grimaced as if she'd just confirmed his worst fear.

She frowned. "Even if my calculations are off a little, this asteroid's still going to hit about as far from human civilization as it's possible to get on this planet, with the possible exception of Antarctica. So what's the big crisis?"

"Okay, here comes the classified part. And for the record, I expect General Fiske doesn't plan to let you out of this hole in the ground until you've signed away your life to him."

A horrible thought occurred to her. "Oh, no!" she exclaimed. "Speaking of my life, I have a lecture this afternoon! My advanced cosmology class—"

Carter interrupted. "Already taken care of. Before you woke up this morning, I asked General Fiske to call the dean of your university. She, in turn, called your department chair, and he assured her the astronomy department will be happy to cover your classes while you're consulting with the government on a highly important and classified project."

A slow grin spread across her face. "I'd pay good money to have seen Bill Kaplan's face after that call. Not only will he be furious that the dean told him to cover for me, but he'll also be going crazy trying to figure out why the government wanted to talk to me and not him."

Carter grinned. "I might have suggested to the general that he make it known to the dean how extremely impressed we are with your research and how disappointed we are that the university hasn't funded your work more aggressively."

"You didn't!" she exclaimed. "You're the best!" She flung her arms around him, and just like that, the atmosphere in the tiny room went from exuberant to crackling with sexual tension. She eyed the door lock wishfully.

Carter stared down at her, his body rigid against hers. Suddenly, she was hugging a marble statue. "Oh, Lordy. I didn't trigger an episode, did I?" she wailed.

"No," he gritted out. "This is me doing my damnedest not to throw you down on the floor and have my way with you."

Oh, yeah. Operation Bed the Hunk was definitely back on track. She asked as casually as she could muster, "Are you sure we don't have time for a little hanky-panky?"

He sighed and dropped a quick kiss on her forehead before taking a step back from her. "Let me finish briefing you and then you decide for yourself."

She tried to gather her scattered thoughts as he perched on the edge of the desk. This was crazy! She lost her mind completely every time he touched her. She had to focus here. Try to at least act marginally intelligent. There was no way she was as accomplished a scientist as he seemed to think, but she had to fake it as best she could.

Was it getting stuffy in here? She paced the room restlessly. It was already starting to feel like a cage. The walls were *not* slowly creeping in on her.

He said heavily, "I took a look at the spot you're predicting the asteroid is going to hit, and there's a little problem with it."

Now what? She stopped pacing and faced him head-on. What had she missed? She cast back over her research. Nothing indicated that even a single human would be hurt when A-57809C landed in a blaze of glory in a few weeks.

Carter continued, "You see, the Russians installed a

remotely operated computer system a few years back right where you're saying the asteroid's going to hit. We in the U.S. government call it the doomsday machine."

"Sounds ominous."

"It is. It's an automated system for launching their entire nuclear arsenal if a certain set of conditions are met."

Apprehension was starting to buzz low in her belly. "What sort of conditions?"

"We believe it'll be a combination of several triggers. Loss of computer or radio contact with Moscow. Loss of external power to the system itself. A nearby impact of sufficient heat and force to simulate a nuclear detonation. An accompanying electromagnetic pulse to verify the nuclear nature of the explosion."

Oh. My. God. She asked in a small, scared voice, "And who will this machine launch the entire Russian nuclear arsenal at?"

"Us."

Chapter 4

Lily's stomach simultaneously turned to stone and dropped all the way to her feet. "This is bad, Carter. Really, really bad." She paced around the small space, wringing her hands, then reversed direction when she started to make herself dizzy. "We have to tell someone. Right away! That asteroid could accidentally set off this doomsday thingie!"

He smiled gently. "I already have told plenty of people. Why else do you think you're here? Uncle Sam wants you and me to run your simulation and verify the accuracy of your predictions, and then we'll figure out what to do next."

She couldn't seem to stop pacing, nor could she seem to pull her scattered thoughts together enough to think.

Thankfully, Carter stepped in front of her, halting her latest lap around the room. He took her icy hands in his warm ones. "It'll be okay, Lily. Thanks to your forecast model, we've got a little time to fix this before something unfortunate happens."

"Unfortunate?" she cried. "It'll be the end of the world! Even if no one fires back at Russia, they'll throw the entire planet into nuclear winter. Whoever doesn't die of radiation will starve!"

"Like I said, we've got some time."

"How can you be so calm about this?" she demanded angrily. "This is horrible!"

"I got my panic out of the way when I first saw your data. And besides, I'm a soldier. I'm trained not to panic."

He was right. She had to calm down. To *think*. She was a scientist. She could come up with a logical way to avoid Armageddon.

"Why don't you sit down, Lily? Have a bite to eat? Clear your head," he suggested mildly.

She flared up, "If you think I can eat at a time like this, you're crazier than me."

He merely shrugged and reached for a piece of bacon. Gradually, his complete calm penetrated her panic and she moved to the desk and started to type into the computer.

"What're you doing?" he asked.

"Signing on to the internet so I can access my files at the university."

"This facility isn't connected to the internet. It's too big a security risk for a place like this. I do, however, have a flash drive with your equations on it. I downloaded them from the internet a few days ago."

Smiling brilliantly at him, Lily gratefully took the storage device he held out to her. She plugged it into the computer and got to work.

Two hours later, she was about to pull out her hair in frustration. The computer they'd given her was too slow, it lacked the right programs to run the calculations she needed, and furthermore, the keyboard typed funny. She needed a decent mainframe, darn it.

"Carter, this isn't going to work," she announced.

He looked up from the laptop someone had brought in for him. She'd put him to work designing a program to cross-check the string calculations that were the basis of her entire theory. He kicked his feet down off the corner of the desk and sat up straight. "What isn't going to work?" he asked warily.

"I need access to real computing power if I'm actually going to run a full simulation of the asteroid strike."

"How much power are we talking?"

She sighed. "I need a full-blown supercomputer array. They don't happen to have one of those stashed down here, do they?"

"Sorry. We're at Camp Nowhere, not the Pentagon."

"Any chance you know where I can get access to a big system?"

"Actually, I do. But we'd likely have to take a little trip," he said.

"I'm up for anything that'll get me out of this salt mine. It is an old salt mine, isn't it?"

He blinked. "How'd you guess?"

"Not too many minerals indigenous to this region have to be mined so deep, and this facility is dry, which eliminates just about everything but salt."

Grinning, he commented, "I forgot for a minute that you're a brilliant scientist."

"I don't know about the brilliant part. Most folks think I'm a certified looney toon."

"That's because they don't understand your work and they don't like feeling stupid. Better to call you crazy than admit you're smarter than they are."

Her eyes widened. That possibility had never occurred to her. "You think?" she asked doubtfully.

"I do. I also think you need to eat something before you pass out on me. You're a tiny little thing and can't possibly store much reserve energy."

Now that he mentioned it, she was getting a decent headache. Reluctantly, she left her calculations and forced down a dry sandwich, a small bag of chips and a soda.

"So, where are you from, Lily?" he asked as she ate. "Your dossier only said Florida. But that's a pretty big place."

"I have a dossier?" she exclaimed. "My God, my parents were right. They've always sworn the FBI was watching us."

"A little radical, are they?" Carter asked wryly.

She shrugged. "They protested the Vietnam War. That's enough to get someone investigated by Uncle Sam, isn't it?"

She thought he reddened a little. "I wouldn't know. A dossier was only prepared on you when I had to brief the doomsday scenario to my superiors. I needed them to respect your credentials and take your predictions seriously."

"Did you tell them I'm a crackpot?"

He laughed. "No, I told them what I told you. That you're brilliant and I think you're onto something."

"With all due respect, how do you know? Not many people have the background to read my algorithms and actually make sense of them."

He shrugged. "I have a little experience with computers. I built a face-recognition program a while back that uses similar algorithms to analyze variations in facial bone structure."

"Where did you learn how to do that?"

"MIT," he confessed.

"You went to MIT? I didn't know they let in good old boys."

He commented lightly, "They let in a few of us crawdad suckers every year to populate the bottom of their bell curves. Makes everyone else feel smart."

She laughed. "They don't let any dummies into that place." So, he wasn't just a hunky grunt after all. "How did you go from MIT to an ambush that nearly did you in?"

His eyes shuttered and she felt his sharp pullback. He answered tightly, "ROTC. My folks had saved for my college, but they couldn't afford to put me through an out-of-state school on their own."

Silence fell between them. Before it could get awkward, she asked, "How's your program to check my work coming?"

"Almost done. How's your pass through your equations coming?"

She shrugged. "Slow. It's hard to see mistakes in my own work. I could use another set of eyes on it."

"You want me to take a look?"

"Have you studied chaos theory?" she asked in surprise.

"Some. My undergrad degree was math. My master's was in computer science."

Well, well, well. A math geek, huh? They might just have stuff to talk about at the breakfast table after Operation Bunk the Hunk concluded. His hotness factor went up, if possible, a few more notches.

"Aren't you just full of surprises," she murmured.

He raised his soda can to her in mock salute. "And to think I can even wrestle alligators."

"Wrestle alligators!" she exclaimed. "Are you insane?"

"Nope. Just a kid from the bayou."

Her gaze narrowed. "Does anyone actually buy that load of hooey?"

His eyes sparkled like blue diamonds. "You'd be surprised how many people do."

"Well, I'm not one of them, mister. You can drop the dumb soldier act with me."

He leaned forward, planting his elbows on the desk, and said low, "Yeah, but you wanted to go to bed with the dumb soldier."

"I want to go to bed with the really smart guy more," she retorted.

He shook his head. "I dunno. That's not generally my experience with women."

"Exactly how many astrophysicists have you dated?"

Skepticism still glittered in his gaze. "We probably should get back to work. After all, the fate of the world is depending on us."

"You can stop saying stuff like that. It's stressing me out too much to think."

He snorted. "Your brain doesn't slow down even when you're unconscious. Did you know you talk in your sleep?"

She started. "What did I say?"

"Something about an operation and a hypothesis. And a short skirt, I think."

Oh, Lordy. "I must have been dreaming," she replied hastily. Eek. Must be careful about her thoughts right before she fell asleep.

"Mmm. Must have," he murmured noncommittally. She looked sharply at him to see if his eyes revealed more, but they were expressionless.

She turned back to her work, inexplicably embarrassed.

What if she'd said more that he wasn't telling her about? That would be bad. Really bad.

Carter had to turn away to hide his amusement. When she'd started mumbling and thrashing in the other room last night, he'd raced to her side to make sure she was all right and no one had broken into the cabin to snatch her.

Instead, there she was, chattering up a storm about Operation Land Sexy Hunk and slinky negligees and red lipstick and mental notes about not acting desperate. It had been so adorable and sexy he'd nearly crawled into bed with her and made love to her right then. But he suspected that if she even caught a hint of him thinking she was desperate, she would metaphorically head for the hills and never come down.

Somehow, he was going to have to make her think she was taking the lead and seducing him. Frankly, he was fascinated to see what she came up with by way of doing so. But for the moment, they had a true crisis on their hands, and it was his job to give her *whatever* she needed to solve it.

He stood up. "I'm going to go speak to the general about getting you more computing power."

She didn't look up from her keyboard and merely grunted an acknowledgment. A strand of silky chocolate hair had fallen over her face, and she was typing too furiously to push it out of the way. He couldn't resist. He reached over and tucked the wayward strand behind her ear, which was as delicate and pink and soft as the rest of her.

He slipped out of the room. As he moved into the hallway, he exhaled hard. Just being in the same room with her stretched him tighter than a high wire. He couldn't remember the last time he'd been so attracted to a woman.

Her combination of innocence and brains was absolutely lethal.

He tried to shake off his improper thoughts of her as he stepped into the general's office, but she was always there, the feel of her lurking in his palms, the sweet taste of her on his lips.

"Captain Baigneaux. How's it coming?"

"Slow. This facility just doesn't have enough computing power for her."

The general looked surprised. "What the hell does she need? The Pentagon's Cray array?"

"She could keep it busy for a couple of hours, I expect."

"The Department of Defense can't just cough up that kind of time. It takes months to schedule a run that big."

"We don't have months. Her calculations show the asteroid hitting in a little over two weeks."

Fiske swore under his breath. "I'll make some calls. See what I can do. But you damn well better be right about this or heads are gonna roll."

Namely, his head. Carter answered grimly, "I'm sure about her, sir. Dr. James knows her stuff. And about that supercomputer access—I may know where she can get some heavy mainframe time elsewhere. If you'll let me make a call of my own first?"

"By all means. I hate to ruin the big brass's day."

Like the general was chump change? Although at the levels Fiske would have to go to to get Lily the computer power she needed, Carter supposed a lousy one-star general didn't pull much weight.

Carter pulled out his cell phone before he remembered it got no signal down here. He excused himself from Fiske's office and went to the comm center to make a secure call.

He stepped into a soundproof phone booth, and in a few moments, his boss, Navy Commander Brady Hathaway, came on the line. Brady commanded the military side of a secret surveillance facility in the Caribbean that was housed inside an extinct volcano. H.O.T. Watch was where Carter had worked for the past few months.

"Boudreau, how's your mission going?" Brady asked warmly when they were connected.

Carter winced. Of all people, Brady knew just how screwed up his former operator was, and just how big a deal it was for Carter to get back out in the field like this, even if it was a simple mission to collect a civilian female and talk to her.

"I'm holding up so far, but it was a close thing in that second attack. Are you sure you want me out here, sir?"

"Yes, I am. Keep an eye out when you're above ground at Camp Nowhere, though. That place has no perimeter fence. It may be remote, but it's open country out there."

"Roger, sir. I'll keep it in mind." Although, he doubted anyone had followed them out here last night. The road behind them had been deserted and dark for hours. They hadn't seen another car for most of the drive.

"Any ID on these Russians?" Brady asked.

"The campus police at the university have all the descriptions they collected from the bystanders. You can get the workups from them."

"Will do." A pause, then Brady asked quietly, "Any more freeze-ups?"

Carter sighed. "I'm okay for the moment. I brought Lily here so I'd have a secure place to brief her in and hide her from the Russians. But we've got a problem. She needs more computer juice than they've got here. What are the odds we can get her access to Big Bertha?"

That was their nickname for H.O.T. Watch's supercomputer array, whose main job was to continuously sort through video surveillance imagery from the entire western hemisphere in search of threats.

"I suppose that could be arranged. I'd have to talk to Jennifer about it."

Jennifer Blackfoot was Brady's civilian counterpart at H.O.T. Watch Ops. She ran all the CIA and other civilian intelligence agents attached to the operation.

Brady continued, "You want to bring your astrophysicist down here?"

Carter frowned. She wasn't *his* astrophysicist. Not by a long shot. He had to admit he liked the sound of it, but the reality was that the good doctor was just impressed by all the secret military stuff and not necessarily him. Belatedly, he mumbled, "I'll bring her to the island if it's necessary."

"It may be. I don't know if we can remote link you to Big Bertha. I'm assuming you want to run simulations of the asteroid impact, but I doubt you'll have the bandwidth at your end to handle that many packets of data per second. Bertha can really pour out the calculations."

Carter was fully aware of just how powerful Bertha was. He was one of the techs who'd helped soup her up over the past several months into the monster she was today. "I'll look into it and get back to you, boss."

"Let me know what I can do for you."

"Thanks."

"And, Carter, good job getting back in the saddle."

He disconnected the call with his boss glumly. Hell, he'd only managed to save Lily by the skin of his teeth. Had he needed to shoot his pistol one more time to save her, she'd be in the custody of the Russians and imprisoned or dead right this second.

Some protector he was. Did he dare take her out of here

under his protection? Or should he call his boss back and ask one of the other operators to take over protecting her? The mere thought of all that crackling sexual energy of hers pouring toward some other man who'd take what she had to offer and not look back made his teeth gnash.

Who was he kidding? He was a mess and she'd be a fool to get involved with him. Hell, he couldn't even keep her safe from a simple assault. If he gave a damn about her at all, he'd step aside and let somebody else take over this mission.

Chapter 5

Lily looked up when Carter stepped back into the little workroom. His expression was stony. "You okay?" she asked.

"I'm fine," he sighed, sounding aggrieved. "But I don't think we're going to be able to run your simulation here. This facility's servers can't handle the data stream from a supercomputer, despite General Fiske's belief that this is the best computer facility in the whole wide world."

She smiled in commiseration.

Carter continued, "The good news is, though, I found us a computer. The bad news is you're going to have to leave the country to get access to it."

Apprehension tightened her gut. "You said I'm going to have to leave the country. What about you?"

"Look, Lily. As much as I hate to admit it, I'm not capable of looking out for you adequately. I'm going to call in someone else to provide security for you."

"But I don't want anyone else!"

"That's sweet of you. But I know some guys…married guys…who can get you where you need to go safely."

"But will they understand the math? Can they help me with my work? Can they act as sounding boards for me when I need to brainstorm something?" she demanded.

"You don't need me for that. You know what you're doing," he replied grimly.

Panic beat at her ribs. "That's not true. I'm not nearly as smart as you seem to think I am. If my theory works, it'll be mostly dumb luck. I need you to check my work and verify it. People's lives are riding on us getting this right."

"There is no us, Lily."

She stared at him in dismay. No them? No Operation Sexy Southerner? "Oh," she said in a tiny voice. "I thought… Never mind. My mistake." She turned away lest he see her disappointment and think she was even more pathetic than he already did.

"Hey." He spoke from directly behind her.

She sniffed, hoping he'd mistake the sound for allergies or something.

"Lily." His hands touched her shoulders, turning her gently to face him. "What's wrong?"

Dear Lord. Please don't let her break down and sob like a child who'd just dropped her ice-cream cone in the dirt. "N-nothing's wrong."

He chuckled lightly. "If I know one thing about women, it's that when they say nothing's wrong, something is *definitely* wrong. Talk to me, sugar."

"I just thought…maybe we…you…" She burst out all in a rush, "Don't you like me? Even a little bit?"

"Excuse me?" He stared blankly at her.

Darn it, did he have to go all dense and man-stupid on her now? She didn't want to have to explain herself.

"Did I come on too strong? Or seem desperate? I mean, I suppose I am desperate. It's not like guys like you come along very often, and certainly not one as hot as you who will give me a second look. Ohmigosh, I can't believe I just called you hot to your face. You're probably insulted… master's degree from MIT…I'm such a dork…"

Two fingers pressed gently against her lips, stopping the flood of babble spilling from her mouth.

"I like it that you think I'm hot. I think you're hot, too."

She stared up at him. No matter how often he said it, she still had trouble believing him. "Really?"

He sighed. "Yes, really. I'm not passing you off to someone else because I don't like you. Hell, I ought to pass you off precisely because I like you too much. But in reality, I'm calling in someone else to look after you because I'm a mental wreck. I don't trust myself to keep you safe, and I care about you too much to let my stupid male ego get you hurt."

"But you did fine back at the campus. You chased off those Russians twice and got me safely out of there."

He shook his head in denial. "It was a close thing both times. I got lucky. You got lucky. I could've gotten you killed. Thing is, I was so determined to get back into the field and prove that I could beat this thing in my head that I put your life in danger. That's unconscionably selfish of me. I won't make that mistake again."

"But I don't want anyone else protecting me," she insisted.

"Didn't you hear what I just said?"

"Yes, Carter, I did. But that doesn't change how I feel. I believe in you."

"But it's not logical," he said desperately.

"You'll do just fine. You thawed right out when I gave you that massage."

He snorted. "It's not like we can call a time-out mid-shoot-out for you to give me a massage before we get back to the fighting."

"No, but it does mean you're capable of coming out of an episode much more quickly than you thought you were. If we can find the right triggers, we may be able to teach your mind to release the muscle spasms in a matter of seconds and not minutes."

He blinked, startled. "What were you doing on the computer while I was gone?"

Busted. She confessed, "This facility has some psychology books in its intranet online library. I did a little reading about psychosomatic events."

He shook his head. "You were supposed to be saving the world."

For a moment, she controlled an urge to stick out her tongue at him as it would be entirely unprofessional. But then she thought better of it and stuck out her tongue anyway. "Tough. I was saving you instead. And you're every bit as important."

"I'll be just as dead as everyone else if Armageddon happens," he declared.

She fired back, "All the more reason to get you fixed now so you can enjoy your last few weeks on earth before you get fried."

"I hate arguing with smart women," he grumbled.

She'd take that as an admission of defeat. The matter of her bodyguard settled, she announced, "I've done about all that I can here. I'm going to need that mainframe of yours to start running simulations."

"Then I have a few more phone calls to make. You and I are going on vacation tomorrow."

She frowned. Vacation? What was he talking about? They had urgent work to do.

He said, "It's probably too late for us to leave the base tonight. I'll ask the general to arrange transport out of here in the morning."

"And where exactly are we going?" she asked, perplexed.

He grinned. "Paradise."

He obviously wasn't planning to tell her any more. He was probably going to whisk her away to another classified military base tucked away in some god-forsaken corner of the planet.

"Can we at least get an office with windows next time?" she asked.

"Sorry. There won't be windows, but they've got the prettiest beaches you ever saw."

Beaches? That sounded distinctly better than a salt mine.

"Let's call it a day, Lily. I don't know about you but I'm beat."

She was feeling a little wrung-out, too. The low-level hum of claustrophobia she'd been fighting all day had taken its toll on her. "Thank God. I'm more than ready to get out this box."

"Sugar, if you needed distracting, you should have told me," he murmured in gentle reproach.

"And there's one more reason I need you as my bodyguard," she declared. Carter led her to the elevator, and her palms actually broke out in a sweat on the long ride back up to the surface.

They'd been in the elevator about a minute when he murmured, "Breathe, *chère*. Ride's almost over."

"How'd you know?" she gritted out from behind her clenched teeth.

"You're white as a sheet."

"Sorry. I've had about all the tight spaces I can stomach for one day."

"I know just the thing to make you feel better."

"Do tell."

"How about I show you instead?"

During the short ride back to their cabin, he said no more about what he had planned. Dinner was waiting for them when they got there. She passed on the thick hamburgers, but dug into a tasty salad. Darkness fell, and the desert heat faded as quickly as the twilight.

"There are sweatshirts in the dresser," he murmured. "Let me get us a couple."

He came back into the living room carrying the quilt from the bed and two giant GO ARMY sweatshirts.

"C'mon," he said cheerfully, hoisting the quilt in his arms. He passed her one of the sweatshirts, and it came down nearly to her knees. He pulled on the other one, and it fit him comfortably. Okay, she felt puny now.

"Where are we going?"

"Where else? Stargazing."

How did he know? Smiling widely, she followed him outside. He made his way around the back of the cabin and led her up a narrow animal trail crisscrossing the massive sandstone outcropping there. In a few minutes, he'd spread out the blanket and they stretched out side-by-side atop a bluff that afforded them an unrestricted view of the entire night sky.

There was no ground light to speak of and the display of stars and planets was magnificent. Short of using a telescope, it was one of the best night skies she'd ever seen.

"I've got to come out to the middle of the desert more often. This is incredible."

"What's your favorite object in the night sky?" he asked in an awed hush beside her.

"I like the Milky Way star band. All those suns and their planets out there. I figure some of them have got to have intelligent life on them," she answered.

He nodded beside her. "I like the stars that twinkle. Why do they do that anyway?"

"Atmospheric interference from the earth makes them seem to twinkle. Some stars that actually do twinkle—pulsars—but they're generally far too faint to see with the naked eye."

They fell silent. She breathed deeply, savoring the vastness of it all, the sense of wonder within her that soared free out here.

"Feeling better?" he asked eventually.

"Yes. Thank you."

"Warm enough?"

She nodded. Although even if she were half-frozen, she wouldn't have admitted it. She didn't want to go back inside yet. She observed, "I think I was born several centuries too soon. I'd give anything to head out there and explore."

"I think you were born at just the right time," he replied absently.

"Why do you say that?" she asked.

"Because this way I got to meet you."

There it was again. The instant and powerful attraction hanging between them. "Would you mind if I asked you a dumb question?"

Carter chuckled. "I can't imagine any question from you being dumb, but shoot."

"Is it always like this with you and women?"

He twitched beside her. "Like what?"

It was her turn to squirm. "You know. All sexy and heavy breathing-ish?"

"Are we breathing heavily? I hadn't noticed."

"I'm serious," she retorted. "I'm the first to admit that I don't have much experience with this kind of stuff. But I don't ever recall this degree of tension between other guys and me."

"Glad to hear it," he rumbled under his breath.

"Well?" she demanded.

He rolled to face her, propping himself up on an elbow to loom over her. "No, smarty pants. It's not always like this. You're special."

"Special as in wonderful or special as in I'm a little thick in the head?"

"You really have to get over this rotten self-image of yours," he declared.

"I'm a scientist, remember? I deal in facts. Fact is, I'm no big catch."

"Fact this, then." His mouth closed over hers and he kissed her slowly and deeply. And oh, my, did she ever like it. He clearly planned to take control of the situation, and she thought that was just perfect. She was sick and tired of neurotic, beta-male academicians being all timid with her. Turned out she didn't like the Woody Allen type after all. Give her Conan the Barbarian or give her no man at all!

Carter might have the muscles, but she had to admit her Conan didn't kiss like a barbarian at all. His mouth moved across hers with finesse, his tongue dipping between her teeth to lick at her like a delicious ice-cream cone. His free hand wandered across her stomach and somehow slipped under her sweatshirt, his palm burning hot against her skin. Or maybe that was her burning up the night like that.

"You've been playing with fire ever since we met," he muttered against her neck. "Time to follow through on all those come-hither looks and flirty little smiles, sugar. If you plan on telling me to stop, do it now."

Or else what? The idea of driving him wild with lust made her head spin. And the stars over them definitely were spinning faster than normal.

"Don't stop," she gasped against his mouth.

"You're sure?"

"Yes, already!"

He laughed darkly. "Then come with me for a ride, little girl. You might be able to take me to heaven, but I can take you someplace much, much hotter than that."

This was a colossal mistake. Carter knew it as surely as he knew he wasn't going to stop unless she asked him to. But it just wasn't in him to turn away from all her sizzling heat. It was wrong to ask her to fix what was messed up in his head. But he'd felt so empty, so broken, for so long. He just wanted to feel whole for once. Deep in his gut he needed to feel alive again. Hell, to feel like a man.

He gathered her close, savoring her smallness and softness against him. She was his polar opposite in every way. His life was defined by self-discipline and focus. Intensity. Seriousness. But she was all about laughter. Imagined possibilities. Embracing life. He used to be like her. He would give anything to be like her again.

And he was selfish and greedy to even contemplate using her to gain all of that back for himself. "We shouldn't do this," he forced himself to mumble.

Her warm hands slid around his neck as she murmured, "Why not? Give me a logical argument."

Logical? Hell, he could barely remember how to spell his name with her pressing up against him like this, all eager sexual intensity. She was making no secret at all of her interest in pursuing a more intimate relationship with him.

He mumbled lamely, "Because we're going to be working together?"

"Coworkers have romances all the time," she retorted immediately against his lips.

Her body undulated against his and his flesh hardened even more. He groaned in near pain. He wanted her so badly that he could barely ungrit his teeth enough to get out, "We hardly know each other."

Her tongue slipped between his lips for a long, lazy taste of him before she murmured, "All the more reason to get to know each other. I may be a ditz sometimes, but I'm not dumb enough to think that a man like you is going to come along more than once in my life. This may be reckless, but I'm not letting you get away from me. I'd never forgive myself if I did."

Her soft belly pressed against his groin, and he'd swear she did it intentionally. His jaw clenched in an effort to control himself. He was a gentleman, dammit. He didn't rip women's clothes off them and fall on them like some slavering beast.

It was as if she picked the thought right out of his brain. "If I asked you to tear off my sweatshirt and have your wicked way with me, would you do it? As a favor to me?"

A favor? He laughed shortly. "Sugar pie, you'd be doing me the favor."

A satisfied smile spread across her face that had his eyebrows climbing in alarm. She drew back far enough to place her hands on either side of his face and gaze deeply into his eyes. "Carter, I need you to do this for me. I want you to rip my clothes off, throw me down and make love to me the way a woman's meant to be made love to. I don't want your logical excuses, I don't want your ever-so-principled insistence on doing the right thing. Heck, I don't even want you to be a gentleman. Can you do that for me?"

His brain froze up right then and there. Complete popsicle. Worse than his body had ever frozen up on him. "I…you…you don't know what you're asking of me," he choked out.

Men like him were careful to keep the strength within them tightly leashed when they were functioning in the real world. But she wanted him to cut it loose? She had no idea what that really meant. She was asking him to free the part of himself that his doctors said he was unconsciously doing his damnedest to bottle up. He had no idea what that part of him would do with a woman in the mix.

She was speaking again, her eyes big and earnest. "…am a grown woman. I have needs and fantasies. And I'm not the kind of woman who usually attracts the kind of man who can fulfill those. But I think maybe you are that kind of man. Am I right?"

"I, uh…" Hell, he couldn't even string a coherent sentence together. "Maybe. Yeah. But…"

"But what?"

He gulped. "You're killing me here. You have to tell me what you want. And you have to tell me if I go too far."

"Take me to that uncontrolled place inside you. That's what I want from you. Share that with me. Show me what I've always been missing in a man."

The woman was deadly. How was a guy supposed to say no to that? Somehow he had to find a way to get control of this situation again. Back away from the abyss yawning so temptingly before him. Could he do it? Could he let her feel his heat without being burned alive by it? No. He wasn't that strong.

But then her hands were on his belt buckle, and damn if her fingers weren't nimble. She had his pants open before he knew what she was doing. Her hot little palm slid down his belly and grasped him boldly. He shuddered in shock.

And the minx smiled up at him sweetly. "Please?"

"You don't fight fair," he gasped.

"Never said I did," she panted back. "The only problem is I didn't get to try out the short skirt or sexy lingerie I had planned. I was really looking forward to those."

The thought of her in a scrap of lace and not much else sent his pulse pounding within her fist. Who'd have guessed the astrophysicist was such a wildcat?

She purred deep in her throat. "Wanna know what else I've always imagined doing with a big strong man like you?"

He laughed painfully. "I hope it involves you getting naked pretty damn soon, or else the guy whose sweatshirts we borrowed is going be plenty mad when he finds them in shreds."

Lily pushed against his chest and he obliged her by rolling onto his back. Like she had in the car, she straddled his hips. But this time, she smiled down at him like some fey creature of the night and reached for the hem of her sweatshirt, drawing both it and her T-shirt over her head by slow inches.

Her body was slim, girlish. But he was coming to learn very quickly that packages could be deceiving. She'd obviously put a great deal of thought into this and knew exactly what she wanted. Far be it from him to disappoint the lady. He gritted his teeth and prepared to do mortal battle with himself.

He reached out for her stomach, enjoying the satin smoothness of her skin. The lower curves of her breasts came into view and he grazed them with the backs of his knuckles, relishing the way her back arched into the light caress. She made a hungry noise in the back of her throat.

Her breasts, revealed by inches, were not large but high and firm and beautifully shaped. Contracting his abdominal muscles powerfully, he sat up to capture the rosy tip of one of them in his mouth and rolled his tongue around the stiff little bud.

As she moaned low, he lay back down. "If you want more of that," he murmured, "you'll have to give yourself to me. I'm not going to just take it."

She smiled broadly. "My pleasure." She leaned forward, bracing herself on the blanket on either side of his head, and presented her breasts to him like candy for the taking. And take them he did. He suckled and nipped and laved the tender flesh until her nipples stood out proudly and she was begging in a raw voice for more.

She wanted to do this with him? So be it.

He surged up, sweeping her into his arms and rolling over, pinning her beneath him. "I can't promise to be gentle," he warned.

"I promise I don't want gentle," she shot back.

He stripped her jeans quickly and, impatient, tore her panties off, too. They gave way with a soft rending of cotton and a less soft sigh of delight from her. The astrophysicist was wilder than he'd ever dreamed.

Carter shucked the rest of his clothes and pushed her thighs wide, splaying her beneath him until she was at his mercy. She trembled, and he checked himself long enough to ensure it wasn't fear but desire making her quake like that. He stroked a finger along her female flesh. It was plump and juicy and ripe and she cried out his name softly. The woman was more than ready for the picking.

But she'd asked for this. Hell, demanded it. And he had plenty of desire for it within him. He cupped his hands under her buttocks, lifting her to his mouth. She gasped and lurched like a man had never taken her this way before. Her former lovers were complete idiots if they had skipped this feast of peaches and cream. She moaned, and then groaned, and then cried out sharply. He relished every last note of her pleasure.

When she was thrashing mindlessly, lifting her hips to him wantonly of her own volition, he shifted his attention to the rest her body, kissing and nibbling his way across her velvet skin, leaving behind a path of trembling destruction in his wake. She was built very small, and he was…not. He needed to make sure she was more than ready to receive him. To that end, he turned her over on her belly and straddled her thighs, holding hers lightly closed with his.

He proceeded to massage her shoulders and back. She seemed perplexed by his change of tactics but enjoyed it, relaxing until she was entirely boneless beneath him. He slid his palms lower, to her pert little tush. It was resilient and round in his hands and he had all kinds of plans for that sweet flesh later. But first, he had to get her to make more of those delicious sounds.

He caressed her skin lightly and she rolled over, giving herself to him without any hesitation or self-consciousness. The trust she showed in him was humbling. He touched her with his fingertips in long, slow strokes that had her writhing madly in moments, begging him to put her out of her misery.

He ground out, "Lily, if you want this, you're going to have to take me."

She didn't hesitate. He was stunned at how quickly she shoved at his shoulders. He obliged her and fell back, sprawling beneath the magnificent blanket of stars overhead.

"You're a bad, bad man, Carter Baigneaux, for teasing me like that."

She threw her leg across his hip and he groaned as all that damp, hot female flesh came into direct contact with parts of him that needed no encouragement at the moment. "But two can play that game," she purred.

He groaned as she rubbed herself blatantly against him but did not close the deal.

"Put your hands flat on the ground and keep them there," she murmured. "And don't move."

He did so, pressing his palms hard against the rock until little bits of gravel dug painfully into them. Up and down his shaft she slid, tantalizingly close to taking him, but oh, so far away. His gaze narrowed, but thankfully, her breath was coming in shorter and shorter gasps, nearly matching his for desperation.

She babbled, "This is incredible… Oh, my…I've never… not like this…" Her hips rocked faster and he began to fear that he was going to crack a molar from clenching his teeth so hard together to hang on while she pleasured herself. Somewhere in the recesses of his lust-hazed mind he registered that she was the most erotic sight he'd ever seen, her body writhing like a siren's, her head thrown back in pleasure, her throat working convulsively as she groaned her pleasure.

And then without warning she lifted herself up and drove downward all in one swift, devastating movement. His entire being froze as her internal muscles clenched him, squeezing and releasing hard and fast around him.

Not now. Surely, his subconscious wasn't so cruel as to give him a seizure now. Panic roared through him. But as his entire body clenched, fighting for self-control, it dawned on him that this felt different. The wrenching agony that usually accompanied one of his freeze-ups was absent.

Instead, blinding pleasure was rolling through him in wave after wave.

Lily drove him mercilessly, insisting he come with her on this journey into magnificent lust. She rode him slow, then fast, easy and then nearly painfully hard. She keened out her pleasure once. Twice. A third time. And all the while he cursed and clutched at the rocks beneath him, doing his damnedest to ride the storm to its very last breath of pleasure.

Finally, it was too much for him. *She* was too much for him. Carter had to move now or die. And shockingly, his body responded. His hips surged up off the ground, meeting her thrust for thrust, slamming into her all the way to her core. Her fingernails dug into his shoulders and her dark hair tossed around them wildly. She was as much a part of the night as the galaxy spinning majestically over her head, and he consumed every last bit of her.

The explosion built so deep within him that he hardly knew its source. With a final climactic thrust, he reached up and grabbed her hips, dragging her down to him with a hoarse cry wrung from the depths of his being. She matched his shout, her release convulsing around him, milking his body and soul until he was so wrung-out that he couldn't breathe.

She collapsed upon him, her body small and light on his. They lay together, breathing in ragged gasps for long minutes. Gradually, she transformed from a powerful sorceress imbued with all the dark power of the night into the light-filled fairy being from before.

He was, quite simply, blown away.

Eventually, she mumbled in a small voice, "Are you all right?"

He laughed, a short snort of disbelief. "You're kidding, right? I think you've killed me."

"Ohmigosh. I didn't even think... Did I hurt you?"

"Good God, no, woman. You pleasured me until I think I'm ruined for any other woman."

"Oh." A pause. "Oh! That's good, isn't it?" she asked hesitantly.

"Yes, madam astrophysicist, Ph.D. and generally brilliant scholar. That's exceedingly good."

"So, then, maybe you'll want to do that again?"

He laughed beneath her. "Let's just say that's a yes. But let me catch my breath first, okay?"

"'Kay."

"And next time I get to be in charge."

"Oh, my," she breathed.

Oh, my, indeed.

Chapter 6

He was ruined for anyone else? Lily snorted. *She* was the one who'd never be able to look at another man again. She snuggled against Carter's side as he pulled the edge of the quilt up and over them both. She could stay right here forever. Let the world end. She was happy.

She was still happy when she woke up some time later. Lying on his sleeping chest and gazing up at the stars overhead, she absently calculated from their current positions that nearly five hours had passed, based on the movement of the stars since they'd come up here.

Gravel rolled somewhere nearby. Some night creature out hunting for its supper, no doubt. Except, abruptly she was aware of Carter. He'd woken up and gone rigid beneath her. His hand lifted slowly from her shoulder to press a warning finger against her lips. What did he hear that she didn't?

Quietly, he pushed the quilt away. Chilly air bit at her

skin and she shivered as his arm slid out from under her head. What was going on? She listened with all her might and heard nothing whatsoever. Which, come to think of it, was a little odd. Deserts were usually noisy places at night, filled with clicks and buzzes and odd chirping noises.

Carter pointed to her and then to a modest tumbleweed a few yards away. He wanted her to get behind it? She nodded tentatively. He rolled to his stomach and pushed himself up to a crouch. looking like a Greek statue come to life with the faint starlight shining off his marble skin.

She sat up in time to catch a furtive movement at the edge of the plateau. Her mind exploded in panic. They weren't alone up here! That was no mouse. That was a man-size shape she'd just glimpsed.

A second shadow joined the first. Had her Russian assailants found them again? How could they have? She was on a supersecret military base. Or more accurately, above one. She thought back frantically. She'd seen no fences when they'd come here. No signs. Nothing to indicate that this was a restricted area. Had the Russians been able to track them somehow and drive right up to their cabin?

That was all the speculation she had time for before Carter's hand moved behind his back, gesturing sharply toward the little tumbleweed bush. He definitely wanted her to hide. This could not possibly be good.

Carter started to ease forward and she moved backward, trying to glide as noiselessly as he, but then she heard a faint intake of breath. She glanced over her shoulder and saw that Carter was completely still. She froze instinctively. What was wrong now?

She glimpsed a shadow moving to their left at the rim of the plateau to flank them. Simple geometry dictated that Carter wheel left to face this threat. But he did nothing. A horrible thought occurred to her. Was it possible? Say it wasn't so. *Not now.*

She reversed direction, easing up close behind him, then she reached forward and tried to move his arm.

"I'm okay," he barely breathed.

What was up, then?

The second shadow started moving to their right. "Hide," he ordered. Carter fell back. Obviously keeping the bad guys in front of them. She looked around desperately, her mind going a hundred miles per hour. There was only that dinky little bush.

"Gun. My pants," Carter breathed.

She glanced around desperately as the silent, deadly shadows crept forward. Where were their clothes? There. In a jumbled pile.

Carter leaped for the closest shadow. She dived for the clothes, rifling through them frantically as the second attacker stood up, emboldened by her isolation.

The bad guy charged her. Carter grappled with his man, and they rolled toward the edge of the bluff. *There. Something hard and heavy.* Desperately, she ripped at the khaki fabric of his pants, turning them right side out and digging for the pocket holding the pistol. But the thing was hopelessly tangled.

Lily whirled as the attacker charged her. Jamming her finger through the trigger guard of the pistol, fabric and all, she pulled the trigger. An enormous explosion knocked her off her feet. She rolled frantically and was just in time to spy Carter and the other man disappear over the precipice. A scream formed in the back of her throat. She regained her feet, seeking her man, pants dangling from her hand.

Peering past the afterimage of the muzzle flash dancing in front of her eyes, she saw that the bad guy was flat on his back. She whirled, terrified. Where was Carter? It was as if some primal, mama bear switch had been thrown in her brain. Protectiveness surged through her. She heard shouting in the distance. The sound of car motors and skidding tires. Somebody'd heard her gunshot. Reinforcements were on the way. Nonetheless, she raced over to where Carter had disappeared and stared downward. She heard rocks sliding, grunting, and then a man's voice swearing quietly. Thank God. Carter.

A male voice shouted her and Carter's names from the base of the outcropping.

She shouted back, "One guy's shot up top and Carter's around the back of the bluff with another man."

She heard more voices. Shouted commands. Thankfully, it sounded like everyone below was going around to assist Carter and not coming up here just yet. And that was a good thing. For it had just dawned on her that she was buck naked.

She called out quietly, "I'm sending your pants down to you. Sorry about the hole."

His voice floated up to her. "No problem."

She scrambled into her jeans and the GO ARMY sweatshirt just before the first soldier burst onto the plateau.

"Everything okay up here, ma'am?" a voice asked from the edge of the plateau.

"I shot a man. He's over there. You might want to check on him."

"Nice shot, ma'am," the soldier commented. "Straight through the heart. Bled out in seconds."

She'd killed a man? Oh, God. Ohgod ohgod—

"It's okay," the soldier commented casually. "You had to."

He was right. She'd had to do it. It had been a kill-or-be-killed situation. A remnant of the fierce protectiveness that had surged in her gut before tickled her mind. *Still*. She'd killed a man. "I think I may have to throw up."

"Normal reaction to a first kill," the kid said blithely.

Great. She didn't need to be a normal killer. She didn't need to be a killer at all. She hadn't asked for any of this.

"Is Carter okay?" she asked.

The soldier muttered into his collar. He must have a microphone of some kind there. "Still pursuing his attacker," he announced.

"You should go down and help them. I'm fine up here. Captain Baigneaux can come get me."

"Roger, ma'am." Maybe the soldier was just accustomed to following orders without question, or maybe he was a little dim. But either way, he turned and trotted down the trail, disappearing from sight.

Carter arrived soon after that. He snatched up his sweatshirt and yanked it on. His slacks had a blackened hole on his right hip, but Lily figured saving his life had been worth sacrificing the pants.

"Everything taken care of?" she asked brightly.

He scowled ferociously and didn't answer. He merely grabbed up the quilt and stalked for the edge of the bluff. She followed behind, perplexed. What was his problem? He stomped down the trail in front of her and barked at the first soldier who reacted to their arrival by momentarily bringing a weapon to bear on them. Lily frowned. The kid was just doing his job. It was no big deal.

But Carter stormed past the soldier and barged into the cabin without so much as an apology. She followed behind him, frowning.

Carter snatched open the desk drawers one after another. "Bastard got my flash disk," he snarled.

She shrugged. "There's nothing on it that couldn't have been pulled off the internet. We didn't make any substantial changes to the equations today because we didn't have enough computer power to run the calculations. It's no big deal."

Carter whirled, incredulous. "No big deal? We nearly died and you shot a man, and you say it's no big deal?"

"All's well that end's well," she replied cautiously.

"Bull."

What *was* his problem?

"We're getting out of here. Now. For all I know there are more Russians out there waiting to jump us. I'm taking you to H.O.T. Watch and surrounding you with every operator they've got. You're not poking your head out of there until we know exactly what's going on with that damn asteroid."

"What's a hot watch?" she asked.

"C'mon. I'm about to show you."

Carter's surly mood didn't improve one bit as he commandeered a Jeep, loaded her in it and tore out of Camp Nowhere. He drove like a man possessed, racing eastward across the desert. The terrain gradually became hilly and then mountainous. And then the glow of a city illuminated the sky ahead of them. Reno maybe?

All the while, Carter was grim. Tight-jawed. Was he actually in a snit because she'd shot the bad guy? The thought of having taken a human life made her violently nauseous to even contemplate, but why was he freaked out about it? He was a soldier.

Finally, as the skyline of what, indeed, turned out to be Reno came into view, she broke the heavy silence. "What's going on? Why are you so tense?"

"Do you have any idea what it's like to be outnumbered, watch the life of your lover flash before your eyes and be unable to do a damn thing to protect her?"

"You did great! You didn't freeze up, and you took care

of your man. And we weren't outnumbered. It was even odds."

"You're not a soldier," he ground out. "You don't count."

"But everything turned out all right. Although I could have done without having to shoot that guy."

Carter's jaw rippled in the dim glow of the dashboard. He didn't seem to share her optimistic view of the night's events. "What?" she demanded.

"I'm done. I can't function in the field anymore. I'm finished as an operator."

"What's an operator?"

"A field operative. A Special Forces soldier."

"Oh. Well, that's not such a bad thing. There are lots of other things a smart, educated man like you can do with yourself. And frankly, I'll worry about you less if you're not getting shot at all the time."

"Says the pot to the kettle," he grumbled under his breath.

She gave up trying to coax him out of his irritation with himself and the entire situation. She turned to look out the window at the garish strip of casinos that mimicked its much bigger cousin down the road in Las Vegas.

Carter drove them directly to the local airport and pulled up at a building attached to a big airplane hangar. He opened her car door for her in grim silence. Even mad as a wet rooster, the guy couldn't stop being polite. It amused her briefly. But then he whirled and stalked inside the building, leaving her to follow in his wake.

By the time she got inside, he was passing a credit card across the counter to a sleepy-looking man. The fellow directed them to a pleasant-enough waiting room while the on-call flight crew was summoned and a sleek business jet towed out of the hangar and prepped to fly. She had to give Carter credit. The guy didn't mess around. When he said they were leaving now, he meant exactly that.

Before long, they were flying south and east into the early morning, headed for she knew not where. In some alarm, she'd reminded Carter she didn't have her passport with her, but he didn't seem to think that was going to be a problem where they were going. Wherever that was. He'd been singularly uncommunicative on that particular subject.

He ordered her gruffly to sleep and then reclined his seat to do the same. She stared at his profile until her eyes burned with fatigue, reminding herself that his complete change of demeanor toward her had nothing to do with the fact that he'd gotten into her pants and was now done with her. But his grouchiness still hurt.

Depressed, she rolled over and allowed herself to drift into restless dreams of blood and dying men reaching out to her in supplication.

She awoke at a brief touch on her shoulder. Carter murmured, "Put your seat up. It's time to land."

Interested, she peered out her window and was startled to see nothing but deep blue water below. As she watched, it shifted in color to a deep teal, and then to a beautiful, vivid turquoise that could only be the Caribbean. Carter had mentioned great beaches, so she supposed that made sense.

The plane bumped onto a runway lined with palm trees and white sand. She spied no buildings on her side of the plane. A huge, dark green mountain rose up beyond the trees, perhaps a half-mile away. Steep and symmetrical, it looked volcanic in origin. The jet taxied clear of the runway, and still she spotted no signs of civilization.

The engines shut down and Carter got out of his seat silently. Still being surly even after his nap, huh? She shrugged and unbuckled. Lily followed him outside into muggy, thick heat and stood back as the copilot closed up the jet.

"Stay here," Carter ordered her. He moved in front of the plane and commenced making hand signals to the pilots. In moments the engines started. Carter waved his hands to guide the plane out of its parking spot. He stood beside her, silent, watching as the jet taxied out to the end of the runway, spooled up its engines to a scream that had her clapping her hands over her ears, and then released its brakes. The plane picked up speed, lifted off and retreated quickly into the distance. Silence fell once more.

She looked around in dismay. They appeared to be stranded in the middle of nowhere. She asked lightly, "So where's the elevator into the cool underground facility?"

"This way."

Seriously? She followed him with interest as he took off hiking into the trees. Once they gained the cover of the jungle, a sandy footpath came into sight, winding through the thick tropical foliage. She was sticky with sweat and strands of hair stuck to her forehead before they emerged from the steam heat of the jungle to a beach.

As promised, it was a truly beautiful little beach in the shape of a crescent moon, ringed by white sand and lapped by lazy blue waves. She could go for a dip in that cool, beckoning water right about now.

Carter followed the curve of the beach and she slogged along behind him, struggling through the deep sand. He rounded the headland and disappeared momentarily from sight. As she rounded the point herself, she came to a startled halt. Was that…

No way. A mini-submarine sat low in the water in front of her, its hatch raised as if it was waiting for them.

"C'mon," Carter said with a little more animation.

She picked her way over the outcropping of sharp rocks to join him.

"I'm going to lift you over to the sub," he announced. His hands went around her waist, and she was passed to a man nearly as large and muscular as Carter who emerged from the interior of the vessel. Carter leaped across the stretch of water lightly behind her, and they descended a ladder carefully to the interior of the small vessel. Large glass panels in its side kept the thing from feeling too much like a tin can about to be crushed by the massive weight of the water around them.

But her breathing still accelerated as the hatch thunked closed and pressure pushed on her eardrums. The submarine submerged perhaps a dozen feet and cruised at that depth for a little while. She could still see rays of sunlight streaking the water outside and was able to settle back and enjoy the fish's eye view of the sea—at least as much as she could while sealed inside a tin can and sunk in the ocean.

"You're determined to freak me out by finding every confined space you can to stuff me in, aren't you?" she accused under her breath.

"You know what they say, exposure's the best cure for a phobia."

She glanced at him sharply. He was right. And that gave her an idea—

But then the submarine came to a halt, distracting her sharply. The driver fiddled with the controls and the vessel performed a slow ninety-degree pivot. It began to submerge at a very steep angle. The sunlight above disappeared in moments and only blackness was visible outside. Something metallic creaked, and panic ripped through her.

"I don't like this," she quavered.

Carter reached over and grabbed her hand. "Look at me," he ordered.

She glanced up at him, eyes wide and heart pounding.

"We're heading into a tunnel. It's not long. It opens into a cave inside an extinct volcano. There's a huge network of tunnels through this island created by lava flows millions of years ago."

"Magma," she corrected absently.

"Excuse me?"

"It's magma when it's underground. Only when it emerges above ground does magma become lava."

"Lava. Magma. Hot, melted rock that carves tunnels and caves out of mountains."

She smiled at his grumpy tone. Maybe he wasn't that fond of tiny dark spaces underwater either. Her own panic receded slightly.

The driver spoke up. "We're almost there. We've begun our ascent into the docking cave. Pirates used to use this place to smuggle slaves and whiskey. They're the ones who supposedly widened this tunnel and smoothed out the walls. Legend has it they hauled barrels of whiskey through here using a system of ropes with men on each end of the tunnel."

The surface of the water came into sight overhead. Artificial light shone down through it. And then the mini-sub broke the surface and she breathed a sigh of relief as Carter popped open the hatch. "Welcome to H.O.T. Watch, Lily."

She took his hand as he helped her up the ladder and stepped out into a giant cave that did look exactly like the kind of place pirates and whiskey smugglers would frequent. "Cool!" she exclaimed.

Carter's hard gaze softened for a minute. "I never get tired of coming into the facility this way." But then he was off, striding toward a black opening in the rock wall in front of them. She tagged along, wishing her legs were a little longer or his a little shorter.

The tunnels were high and brightly lit enough not to make her feel too closed in. After the submarine, they were a huge improvement. She consoled herself with the notion that she was probably very close to the surface.

And then Carter stepped out into a massive room that made her breath catch in her throat. It was the size of an outdoor drive-in movie theater in here. The place was easily a hundred yards long and a good fifty feet tall.

"This was the main magma chamber when the volcano was active," Carter murmured.

Voices called out greetings to Carter from computer stations in long rows of high-tech consoles pretty much covering the floor of the cave. A raven-haired beauty came down a set of metal steps from a glass observation room high on one wall of the cave. Lily didn't think of herself as the jealous type, but it was hard not to have her gut tighten at the warm smile the woman gave Carter.

"Lily, this is Jennifer Blackfoot. She runs the civilian side of the house around here."

Lily managed to smile back at the woman's pleasant greeting. "Welcome to the Bat Cave, Dr. James. I hear you need to use Big Bertha."

"Excuse m-me?" Lily stammered.

Carter grinned. "Bertha's our mainframe computer."

Lily nodded in comprehension and smiled at the other woman. "Thank you so much for letting me run my little simulation."

Jennifer laughed. "No, no. Thank you. You're the one who's going to save the world. I'm happy to help."

She really wished people would quit saying stuff like that to her.

"The mountain locked down?" Carter asked gruffly.

"As soon as you cleared the airlock."

"How many operators do we have in-house?" he demanded.

"All of Alpha and Bravo squads. Sixty-plus men. The Medusa and Charlie squads are out on ops right now and couldn't be recalled."

Lily didn't have the faintest idea what they were talking about, but Carter's shoulders relaxed and the grim set of his mouth eased a little.

"How're you doing?" Jennifer asked him quietly. "We retrieved telemetry of the attack on the bluff last night. I was pleased to see your performance." As Carter's gaze went thunderous, she added hastily, "I mean your ability to fight without freezing up."

As Carter continued to be board-stiff beside her, Lily's gaze snapped to Jennifer and she demanded, "How did you manage to get video of us? We were out in the middle of nowhere."

The other woman swept a hand toward three gigantic television screens mounted high on the far wall. "From here we can monitor almost every square inch of the planet at a moment's notice. This facility sorts and monitors inputs from satellite cameras all over the world."

Holy cow. Her parents' wild theories about government surveillance from space were true after all! Ha. And people thought she was crazy for believing them. Little did they know.

Carter spoke briskly. "Lily's going to need a workstation. Access to the computational algorithms. Internet access to download her preliminary equations. Those Russians last night stole my flash drive with the equations."

"They caught the second guy, by the way," Jennifer announced. "And we've recovered the flash drive."

"He say anything interesting about who he's working for?" Carter asked grimly.

"He's not talking yet. But the day is young."

Lily jerked at the bloodthirsty chill underlying the woman's mild comment.

Carter nodded. "Let me know what he says, eh?"

"Wilco, Boudreaux."

Lily didn't like the easy familiarity between the two of them. But all jealousy aside, they were colleagues. And it wasn't like either of them was making bedroom eyes at the other. She was just being paranoid. And as much as she might like it to be otherwise, she didn't own Carter.

"We've freed up the station beside yours, Carter," Jennifer was saying. Lily followed along as Carter made his way down a long row of computer workstations.

"This is my desk," he announced. "You can work here, Lily." He gestured at a station to his right.

Lily sat down gingerly at a computer nicer than the best one the astronomy department had back at the university.

"You'll need a password," Jennifer said briskly. "I took the liberty of setting one up for you."

Lily took the piece of paper the woman handed her and typed in the random sequence of letters and symbols when prompted to do so. In moments, she'd connected to the internet and accessed her equations. Comfortable for the first time in hours, she immersed herself in downloading the information and re-creating the tweaks she'd wanted to make to the equations yesterday. She registered that Carter sat down at his own computer and started typing.

After a while, he announced from beside her, "Big Bertha's ready to go. Whenever you're ready to make a test run, I've got the interface set up."

She nodded. "I'm ready. I've created a false data set of easy numbers to work with. If we run this set through and get reasonable results, then we can make a run with A-57809C's numbers."

Carter made an announcement that echoed through the huge cave on a loudspeaker, something to the effect of Bertha going offline for the next several minutes. If all went well, the run should take no more than three minutes. She hit the send button.

A slowly spinning wheel came up on her computer screen. And now the waiting began. A few techs from nearby migrated over to stand behind her at her desk. Before long a small crowd had gathered. And with each added person waiting expectantly, her nerves increased.

"It's not going to be that impressive," she murmured. "Just a bunch of numbers."

"Actually," Carter replied, "I took the liberty of creating an algorithm to translate your calculations into a pictorial image of the impact point and blast pattern of your hypothetical asteroid."

Her eyebrows shot up. That was a heck of a tough algorithm to just whip up. Why hadn't she thought of doing it herself?

Three minutes passed. Four. Her palms started to sweat. Was something wrong with her equations? Had the computer gotten stuck in a computational loop? Frantically, she tried to figure out what she'd done wrong. And then, without warning, the big screen in the middle of the room lit up. A graphic depiction of planet Earth flashed before their eyes, and a small object tracked inbound rapidly, a red arc tracing its progress. The flashing white dot impacted at the North Pole, and bits of debris flew up into space.

Immediately, the view shifted to a close-up image. Green, wavy lines radiated out into the atmosphere, depicting the shock waves. Red, wavy lines spread outward in an expanding doughnut from the impact point, presumably painting the electromagnetic pulse. The view zoomed in even more, and a crater was depicted in a green field of simulated ice.

Applause erupted around her. Okay, so Carter's visual depiction of the impact was pretty cool. But when she thought about the real asteroid and what all those lines and impacts meant, her blood ran cold. If she was right, the worst-case scenario was indeed hurtling toward them through space at this very moment.

"Check this out!" somebody called.

On the right-hand jumbo screen, a fuzzy white dot appeared in the middle of the black screen. The view hitched and the dot grew a little larger. It hitched again and a lump came into view. She recognized it immediately. She'd looked at that asteroid through the university's optical telescope a few months ago just for fun.

The room went silent. Sober. Apparently, everyone here had already been briefed on the implications of that chunk of iron smashing into Siberia and faking out a doomsday system into annihilating them all.

"Where's that picture coming from?" she asked.

"We turned one of the satellite cameras to have a look at it," Carter answered.

"Can you get any higher resolution than that?"

"Nope. That's it. But as the asteroid comes closer, we'll get a clearer picture of it. Why?" he asked.

"I should be able to refine my measurements of its dimensions and estimate its mass more closely from these images. That should help us get a more accurate idea of where it's going to land and when."

"You heard the lady," Carter said to the group at large. "If anyone has any bright ideas for getting a better look at that rock, you're green-lighted to try."

Somebody said from the back, "Why not contact NASA and get them to point the Hubble telescope at it?"

Lily snorted. "The Hubble's booked years in advance."

Jennifer Blackfoot grinned back. "Yeah, but we're H.O.T. Watch. And the fate of the world rests on this."

Lily shook her head. "I'll be grateful for any more imagery you can get me, but good luck with that."

Jennifer murmured something about having a few phone calls to make and wandered off toward her glass office. The other techs scattered back to their desks. The simulated image of the North Pole went away, and a rather bland schematic of sine waves circling the equator came up on the three big screens. She recognized satellite tracks.

Carter said, "We can take Big Bertha offline again in twelve hours for another run."

She nodded. "I'll be ready. If I can get access at my station to the image you just flashed up of the asteroid, I'll take a stab at updating its mass and velocity."

"Roger." He sent her the information and then got up and left his station, leaving her alone.

She spent the next six hours refining her estimates. Her head began to ache and her vision grew blurry before she finally pushed back from the desk. She asked the guy on her right, "Is there a drinking fountain around here? I'm feeling a little dizzy."

"Yeah, sure. Hey, have your gotten up from your station since you got here?" the fellow asked.

"Uh, no. I guess not."

The guy huffed. "I'll call Carter."

She listened with chagrin as the man said into his headpiece, "Boo, your girl's about to pass out down here. Have you fed her in the past day or so? You know these scientists. All brains and no common sense."

She ought to resent the comment, but in fairness couldn't dispute its accuracy. Carter materialized beside her in a few moments. "C'mon, Einstein," he muttered. "Let's get you something to eat and drink."

Glaring at his back, she followed him down a tunnel to a compact cafeteria. He made her sit down while he fetched her a big plate of fried rice and sautéed vegetables, then set two bottles of water in front of her and made her down one of them before she did anything else. As she dug into the rice, he glanced under the table at her feet.

"What're you doing?" she asked around a mouthful of broccoli.

"Checking to see if your shoes are tied."

"Very funny," she retorted. "You're the one who said this was a crisis. I was working as hard as I could to help fix it. If I'd known you wanted me to slack off, by all means I would have done so."

He sighed. "You can sheathe your claws. I wasn't being critical of your work ethic. We appreciate your assistance."

"Do you know if Jennifer's having any success getting access to a telescope somewhere? I told her it doesn't have to be the Hubble. Any of the big observatories can get a good look at our rock now that it's getting close to Earth."

He frowned. "It may be twenty-four hours before we can get you your pictures and radio imaging."

"That's amazing. I gather you guys here are pretty important?"

He shrugged. "I suppose. We're the eyes and ears of the United States in a good chunk of the world."

"So who all works here?" she asked.

"A bunch of linguists and photo analysts. Plus a crew of computer and satellite technicians."

"And Special Forces operators."

He sighed. "Yeah. And operators. This is their operational support headquarters."

Whatever that meant. She'd take it to mean this was their home base or something like that. She shrugged. "Where did you go this afternoon?"

"To talk to some of those operators."

"What do trained killers sit around and talk about anyway?"

He scowled. "Shockingly normal stuff. The wives and kids. Sports. What's in the news. I suppose you professors sit around talking about quantum theory and the nature of the universe."

She shrugged. "Sometimes. Office politics and gossiping about our students are popular topics, too."

Silence fell between them as she finished her meal and downed the second water bottle.

"I'll show you your quarters," Carter announced brusquely. In short order he'd led her down yet another tunnel to a small room that reminded her of what a personal module would look like on a spaceship. But it wasn't like she had, oh, any possessions with her. A bed pretty much did it for her needs.

"Jennifer sent over some clothes and supplies. I put them away for you," Carter said.

She opened the top dresser drawer and saw several articles of clothing folded neatly inside.

"Toothbrush, soap, towels and the like are in the second drawer," he murmured. "There's a shelf of books if you get bored, and a television's behind this panel over here. We get pretty much any channel you want."

"Satellite reception's good down here, huh?" she commented drily.

"Something like that." He looked away and back at her. "Do you want to rest before tonight's run on Bertha?"

"Uh, sure," she mumbled. What she wanted to do was break through this stupid wall he'd put up between them. To throw him down and make love to him again. And this time to convince him to do some of the things with her that he'd only hinted at last night.

"I'll come and get you an hour before the offline window." And then he was gone and she was staring, frustrated, at a closed door.

She turned to explore the tiny room and was delighted when a waist-high panel folded down into a small desk with a laptop sitting on it. She cranked it up and grinned when her password let her onto the system *and* onto the internet. It was time to do a little exploring about one Carter Baigneaux, Captain, U.S. Army, and his little problem. He might have had the best in military medical care, but she was hooked into research networks all over the world. Surely somebody, somewhere, was looking into psychosomatic illnesses and their cures.

Several hours later she leaned back and rubbed the back of her neck to ease the tension there. As she'd suspected, landmark work was being done in Sweden with forcing victims of his type of affliction to confront the source of their trauma. Psychiatrists there were inundating their patients with graphic visual and audio images and desensitizing them to their triggers. It was an extreme approach, but it was showing promising early results. She was no shrink, but she knew a few good ones. Maybe after this mess was over, she could arrange for one of them to talk with Carter about joining the Swedish research project.

She still had an hour to kill before he came to fetch her. It was only early evening, and she didn't feel like sleeping yet. Idly, she typed Carter's name into the computer's search engine.

A list of hits scrolled down the screen, startling her. She'd have thought a Special Forces man like him wouldn't show up much in a public forum like this. She scanned the first page of hits, and they all dealt with something that happened in East Africa some months back. She clicked the first one.

A news article popped up on the screen. "U.S. Army team slaughters children in Sudan," the headline shouted.

She lurched. *What?*

She read on. It seemed a journalist had been embedded with a U.S. expeditionary force that had crossed into Sudan covertly. According to the article, a small team of U.S. commandos had sneaked out of camp one night, and the reporter followed them. They'd swept through a village and then out into the bush. The guy caught up with them in time to witness them mowing down nearly a hundred little boys between the ages of six and fourteen who appeared to have fled from the massacre of their mothers and sisters.

Cold horror washed through Lily. Memories of her parents screaming at political rallies about baby killers flashed through her head. Was it true after all? Was her government that heartless? Was Carter a murderer of *children?*

She scrolled down and abruptly reeled back from the computer screen. Gruesome images of dead boys lying broken and bloody on the ground splashed across it. Dear God. They were *babies,* their faces so sweet and innocent in death.

Sick to her stomach, she read on. How the reporter had circled back and found evidence of the recent massacre in the village the American troops had just gone through. While the reporter couldn't say with certainty that the team, led by one Captain Carter Baigneaux, had perpetrated the horrendous mutilation and murder of the villagers—mostly women and small children—he wrote that it was impossible to conclude otherwise. And the team had apparently raced out into the bush, chasing after the children the villagers had sent away to hide. When the Americans found the children, witnesses to the slaughter in the village, the soldiers had murdered them to the last child.

Lily bolted for the bathroom, emptying the remains of her supper into the toilet in violent wretches. How could she have ever fancied herself attracted to such a monster? God, she'd made love with him? A sudden need to bathe overcame her, and she climbed in the shower and turned it on as hot as she could stand. She let the water pound at her until her flesh was red and tender, but still it didn't erase the feel of his hands on her skin.

She'd gotten out of the shower and dressed and had a towel turbaned around her hair when a quiet knock at her door made her lurch in horror. It was *him*. The baby killer. "Who is it?" she called through the door without opening it.

"It's Carter. Bertha's yours at 10:04."

She glanced at her watch. "Got it. I'll be there."

"Do you want something to eat before then? The cook kept the kitchen open for you."

"No. I'll just meet you on the big floor."

"Uh, all right." He sounded perplexed. Tough. She wasn't spending any more time with him than she had to until she got out of here and as far away from him as she could humanly get.

She paced her tiny room until she was half-crazy, and then she got on the internet again and read a few more of the damning articles. Most of them seemed based off that first article and quoted it more or less verbatim. The pictures were all the same ones with piles of children's bodies, staring in reproachful death at the photographer. When the main articles petered out, she ran into a second set of articles mentioning the journalist for a possible Pulitzer Prize for his exposé.

About twenty minutes before her window of opportunity to do the run on Bertha, she made her way down to the main cave. Thankfully, a number of technicians were there to witness the real run and she didn't have to be alone with Carter. Jennifer Blackfoot was present, along with a tall, grim-looking man who introduced himself quietly as Brady Hathaway. Carter's boss.

Lily avoided looking at Carter as she approached his desk. The images of what he'd done to those children fresh and sickening in her mind, she half turned away from him and did her best to put him entirely out of her mind so she could actually work.

She took one last look through her equations and plugged in her latest information on the asteroid. And at 10:04 p.m. exactly, Carter pointed to her from his desk. She hit the send button. Here went nothing.

Chapter 7

Carter was a mess. He prayed Lily's calculations were wrong, but feared they weren't. He desperately hoped that the projected damage from this particular asteroid wouldn't be severe enough to trigger the doomsday machine. But even more than that, he wanted to know why in the hell the only time Lily had made eye contact with him since she'd gotten down here she'd looked at him like he was the anti-Christ.

As if that weren't enough to drive a guy half out of his mind, he damn well didn't want to have the conversation that was waiting for him after this run of Lily's simulation was complete. Brady had cornered him on the way in here and murmured that he wanted to chat about Carter's performance up on the bluff last night when the Russians had jumped him and Lily.

Not only was the boss going to ream him out completely for sleeping with the astrophysicist, but Brady must have seen the footage of him having to hand one attacker over to a civilian—and totally unprepared. Any self-respecting operator ought to be able to defend against two aggressors. He was done both as a Special Operator and as an officer.

And then there was Lily herself. He'd been furious with himself last night, but he feared he'd taken it out on her. Unfairly. He owed her an apology. She was so quick to blame herself for everything. He'd have to work on her self-confidence— He broke off. That implied a long-term relationship between them. Was he ready to commit to that? Was *she?*

And one thing he did know: he wanted to make love with Lily again so badly that he could hardly see straight. But he was not some randy teen who couldn't think past his fly. Damned if the only thing he saw every time he closed his eyes was Lily, writhing on top of him like some magical spirit of the night, Lily wiggling her tush at him and daring him to do naughty things to her, Lily's eyes closed in ecstasy as she keened her pleasure to the stars above.

Appalled, he yanked his attention back to the blank screens high on the wall in front of him. Any minute now.

An outline of the Earth popped up on the jumbo TV. Everyone gathered around him and Lily inhaled sharply. Here it came. A white dot arced down toward the slowly spinning image of the planet, its course traced by a red line. An outline of the Asian continent spun into view. The asteroid sped across the Earth's surface and plowed into central Siberia exactly as Lily had forecast. His gut clenched in horror as the computer began generating seismic wave lines, a powerful electromagnetic shock wave, and an oblong crater in the permafrost.

It was *exactly* as she'd predicted. Every last condition necessary to set off the doomsday machine was going to be met.

"Looks like your girl was right," Brady commented from behind him.

"Uh, gentlemen?" Lily spoke up grimly from beside him. "We've got a little problem."

"What's that?" Brady asked.

Carter looked over at her, and she was staring fixedly at her computer screen. Mathematical computations sprawled across it. When she glanced up at him, her face was ghostly white. Alarm blossomed in his gut. He might not have known her long, but he knew her well enough to be dead sure that she was a courageous woman. It took something bad—really bad—to put that kind of terror in her big brown eyes. He half rose out of his seat. "What's wrong, Lily?"

"I was wrong about when the asteroid's going to hit."

"How wrong?" he asked evenly, his stomach churning all of a sudden.

"We don't have two weeks. We have more like a week. Maybe less. I'll need to get a really accurate magnetic scan to pinpoint a time frame."

Carter sat down hard. Brady took an involuntary step forward. It went dead silent all around them as everyone stared, frozen.

"Come again?" Jennifer finally choked out.

"The asteroid's going to hit Earth in a week or less." As the thunderous silence continued around her, Lily added somewhat desperately, "I was wondering how you were managing to get such good pictures of the asteroid. I mean, I know your satellites are powerful and all, but I work with some pretty hefty telescopes myself, and I haven't even come close to getting images like you all were able to pull in."

"How is this possible?" Brady half whispered.

"The initial calculations of mass, density and velocity made by the astronomers who discovered the asteroid were wildly incorrect. I analyzed your spectroscopic images and realized the entire asteroid is made of iron, not just ice as was originally assumed. The astronomers thought the tail coming off it was ice vapor. But it's iron particles. And the tail isn't white. It's gray metal reflecting sunlight back at us. This thing weighs close to twenty times what we thought it did. Which means it's coming in much, much faster than anyone previously guessed, and it's going to make a much bigger bang when it hits."

"How big?" Carter demanded, his heart in his throat.

"It's not an extinction-level event, if that's what you're worried about," she said hastily. "We're still talking only regional effects from this thing. It's just that the blast radius, EMP pulse and seismic effects are going to affect an area roughly a hundred times as large as I originally forecast."

Carter leaped to the next logical conclusion for her. "So even if our intelligence about the exact location of the doomsday machine is off a bit, we're now pretty much guaranteed to set the thing off if we're even in the ballpark as to where it's located."

Lily looked at him miserably. "That's correct."

"Translation?" Jennifer asked tersely.

Lily replied, "If the doomsday machine were in, say, Denver, we originally believed the asteroid would have to hit somewhere in the Denver metropolitan area to set it off. But we were wrong. Given how big the impact's actually going to be, the asteroid only has to hit somewhere in the state of Colorado to set off the doomsday machine. Or possibly only somewhere in the Rocky Mountains."

Another heavy silence fell around them.

"Crisis team to my office. Now," Brady said quietly.

Carter stood and looked down at Lily. "That's us."

"I'm on a crisis team now?"

"You *are* the crisis team, sugar."

She winced when he used the endearment and her gaze slid away from him. What was up with that? She might have been mad when he got all huffy at himself after last night's fiasco, but this was a whole new level of distance in her reactions to him.

He led her up the metal stairs to Jennifer's office and through it into the conference room that sat between her office and Brady's. Carter managed to maneuver so he could murmur in her ear, "You okay?"

"No, I'm *not* okay," she muttered back.

He got the impression she was referring to more than the disastrous estimate of impact time. But what?

Brady didn't waste time dithering. When the squad leaders of the two Special Forces teams in the bunker were seated, along with Jennifer, a couple of lead technicians, Lily and himself, Brady said simply, "Now what do we do?"

Bravo Squad leader said grimly, "There's not enough time to deploy a team to Siberia to disable the doomsday machine."

"We've already been over that," Jennifer retorted. "My source was clear on the subject—the odds of you disabling it without kicking off some sort of fail-safe device were nil anyway."

Alpha Squad leader leaned forward. "I don't think we have any choice. We have to talk to the Russians."

Carter bit out, "You mean the same Russians who are doing everything in their power to kill Lily and silence her?"

"Yes," the soldier replied tersely. "Once we tell them

what we know, they'll realize it's too late to silence Dr. James. The fox is already in the hen house, as it were."

"It's a hell of a risk. With *her* life," Carter retorted.

The guy shrugged. "How many people die if we don't convince the Russians to turn off their machine while this asteroid makes landfall?"

Carter all but growled like a wolf. "She's a civilian."

"She's a human being," the guy snapped. "We're talking about possible extinction of the human race here, Boudreaux."

It was all he could do to stay in his seat, not to jump up and pace, not to put his fist through the nearest wall in sheer frustration. And then the unthinkable happened. His leg muscles started to clench up. His back started to go rigid. Quickly, he placed his hands in his lap in what he hoped looked like a natural position. His shoulders began to lock up. He looked up and saw Lily staring at him fixedly.

She stunned him by saying to Brady, "I don't mean to be rude, and it's probably some terrible breach of protocol, but could I have a moment alone in here with Captain Baigneaux? I need to run something past him. It's devilishly complicated math and the rest of you will distract me."

Everyone stared at her blankly.

"Please?" she insisted politely. "It'll take just a minute. Indulge the crazy professor."

Brady stood up, frowning. "You heard the lady. Everyone out."

When the door closed behind the last person, Lily turned to him quickly. "Is this room soundproof?" she demanded.

"Yes. Why? You planning to jump my bones in plain sight of everyone downstairs?"

"No, you many-colored creep. I'm planning to tell you exactly what I think of you before you unfreeze."

He watched her warily. So far only large muscle groups were affected. She turned to face him. "I read about your little mission in Africa. No wonder you said you're going to hell. After what you did, I sincerely hope you do go straight there."

Comprehension broke across him like scalding water. Ah, God. That damned article. Surely the nastiest piece of yellow journalism ever printed. Twisted half truths and lies. All of it. Yes, they'd killed a bunch of boys, but those *boys* were vicious psychopaths, raised practically from infancy to be brutal, inhuman killers. The original Lost Boys of Sudan were grown up now and training a possibly even more sick and psychopathic generation of boy soldiers to do their terrible work. Those were the boys he and his men had killed. But that bit got completely left out of the article of course.

"And those villagers," Lily continued, her voice thick with disgust. "How could you?"

But they hadn't! He and his men had come upon the village after the boy soldiers had gone through the place and wreaked their despicable brand of chaos upon those poor people.

"It's not what it seems. I *swear.*" Hey! He could talk! And if he wasn't mistaken, the leg cramps were already easing. Hallelujah. Was he finally beating the seizures?

"So here's the deal, Carter," Lily snarled. "I know your dirty little secret. And I'll never forgive you for it. But I have a job to do, and like it or not, you're the best person in this joint to help me. I'm going to set aside my contempt for your homicidal tendencies for the next two days and work with you. But once this thing is over, I never want to see or hear from you again as long as I live."

He'd felt pretty helpless during a few of his episodes. He'd thought that had been as bad as it could get. But this was worse. To have her think this of him…not to be able to explain…not to be able to set the record straight…to see the hatred and revulsion in her eyes…no, this was worse.

"It's not true, Lily," he rasped. "None of it."

"I do not want to hear it. I don't want to talk about it. I don't want any of your lies or lame explanations. There's no justification for killing children. Ever."

He froze, stunned. In an instant it hit him with the power of a revelation that, in his heart, he agreed with her. There was no justification for killing children. There had to have been another way to deal with that violent child army besides mowing down a bunch of horribly misguided kids. Maybe they could have been saved. Rehabbed. Given a chance at a new life somehow. But no one would ever know because he'd given his men the order to fire and then unloaded his own fully automatic weapon into those cherubic faces. His head told him he'd made exactly the right call, but his heart didn't buy it.

"What calculations did you need to discuss?" he asked tiredly. Suddenly he felt a hundred years old. His body ached all the way down to his soul.

"There are no calculations. I saw you start to freeze up and thought you might need some time to thaw."

"That's me," he commented wryly. "The human popsicle."

She pursed her lips but made no reply. The ready humor that had spiced up their interactions before was gone. She turned away and opened the door to Brady's office. "Okay, folks. You can come back in."

The group filed back into the room while Carter tried to think up some impressive equation to scribble on the whiteboard by way of explanation for that past few minutes locked in here alone with Lily. But she startled him by speaking up first.

"Carter and I have run the odds, and there's really only one option. He has to take me to the Russians. Together, we have to convince them to turn off their doomsday machine. I doubt they'll leave it turned off, but this asteroid's got to get safely to Earth before they bring it back online."

Jennifer sighed. "The Russians steadfastly refuse to admit that the machine exists, let alone that a necessity might exist that requires it to be disabled."

"Then I guess we'll just have to convince them we're right," Lily replied, "whether they want to admit it to us or not."

Brady added, "What you're suggesting could be dangerous."

"Whereas sitting around doing nothing and just letting this thing kill us all isn't dangerous?" Lily retorted.

"I'm not the guy for the job," Carter interjected. "You need someone who can take care of you—"

"It's you or I refuse to help," she snapped back.

"Why me?" Carter challenged. Surely after her earlier accusations she would want someone else to take over bodyguard duty for her.

"Better the known evil than the unknown one," she snapped back.

Jeez. Not only did she think he was a baby killer, apparently she thought all soldiers were baby killers. He sighed and reminded himself grimly that she was an American citizen entitled to believe whatever she wanted.

Brady frowned back and forth, obviously perplexed by the complex dynamic vibrating between them at the moment. Special Operators were astute judges of people and their behavior, and he was obviously having a hard time figuring out what was up with them. Hell, Carter was confused, and he was part of the whole mess.

"Who do you propose to talk to?" Brady asked Lily.

"I don't know. The powers that be. Someone in the Russian executive branch, I suppose. I could approach some of my astronomer counterparts and let them work their way up through the system to whoever controls the doomsday machine, but a week may not be enough time for that if I understand their academic bureaucracy correctly."

Brady snorted. "To say nothing of the layers of government bureaucracy you'd have to wade through."

"How about we arrange a meeting at the Russian Embassy in Washington?" Jennifer suggested. "Ambassador Dogorovich can get the ear of the prime minister quickly if he needs it."

"It's worth a try. If nothing else, maybe we can pull some strings at the Pentagon and open up a back channel through their military. Whatever we do, it has to happen at light speed," Brady replied.

Jennifer nodded. "I think our best bet is to get these two to D.C. At least we'll have access to the highest levels of our own government if need be to make something happen."

Brady turned to one of the men down the table. "How soon can we have a plane ready to fly to Washington?"

"An hour."

And so it was for the second time in a single day, Carter found himself climbing onto a business jet with Lily and whisking up into the night this time. He waited until the plane was safely airborne and she was a captive audience.

"Listen, Lily. About that article. That reporter didn't tell a fraction of the real story. He took what happened and twisted it wildly out of proportion."

"I saw the pictures, Carter. Are you telling me he faked those?"

He huffed. "No. Those were real. Although it was fascinating how all of the weapons those kids were pointing at me and my men disappeared before the pictures were taken."

"Did you or did you not kill a bunch of children?"

"We did. But—"

"But nothing. Discussion over."

"You're a scientist. How can you refuse to hear the rest of the facts? You're not telling me you blindly believe everything you read in the news or hear on television, are you?"

"Of course not," she replied, a shade indignantly.

"Then why won't you entertain the possibility that this guy wasn't entirely factual in his representation of what happened?"

She sighed hard. Folded her arms defensively over her chest. "Fine. Tell me what really happened."

As he'd already done more times than he could count with various counselors and doctors over the past year, he relayed the details of that awful, unforgettable night. How his team had gotten a report of a massacre in progress. How they'd rushed to the village but had been too late. How they'd tracked the perpetrators and been stunned to stumble upon a child army of emotionless monsters. How the children had closed in on them. Been ordered by their leader to capture the American soldiers and torture them. How a reward had been offered to the children who could keep one of the Americans alive the longest after dismembering them.

And then, painfully, he told her about looking into the eyes of those children and seeing nothing at all. No feelings, no humanity. No *souls*. And that had been when he'd made the kill-or-be-killed decision and given the order to shoot.

"How did giving that order make you feel?" Lily asked in a hush when he finished.

He frowned. "I didn't feel anything. It was the right decision. My men are not monsters. We only kill when it's necessary, and that was a shoot-or-die scenario. I judged that the world would be a better place, safer for the locals, if those children died and we lived instead."

"But afterward? Didn't you feel anything?"

He grunted. "Yeah. I puked my guts up. Couldn't eat or sleep for days. When we got back to our home base, the docs had to drug me into oblivion. When I woke up, I couldn't move a muscle. I stayed that way for two weeks. Plenty of time locked inside my mind to think about the faces of those kids both before and after I shot them."

"And what did you decide?"

He looked away. Back at her. "Look, if you want some big confession out of me, don't hold your breath. I did my job. My men are alive. I don't regret that. I'd make the same decision again."

"Then why do you freeze up every time you get even the slightest bit stressed out?"

"Apparently, the unconscious human brain doesn't deal well with the idea of killing children, no matter how justified it might have been. Or so say the legions of therapists and doctors who've treated me."

She looked skeptical. "Well, obviously they haven't gotten it right yet if you're still having your episodes. They've missed something important."

He replied bitterly, "By all means, if you find it, let me know. Despite your optimistic take on how much worse my life could be, this one still sucks."

She subsided, staring out the window thoughtfully. It

occurred to him she hadn't commented at all on whether she bought his version of the events of that terrible night. Tension coiled in his belly. She had to believe him. He was telling the truth!

The military had done a thorough investigation and completely cleared him and his men of any wrongdoing. Of course, because of the highly classified nature of their team, the government couldn't even acknowledge that any U.S. soldiers had been in Sudan that night, let alone come out with a public statement of support for him and his team.

As the minutes passed and Lily made no move to speak any more with him, he finally turned away and reclined his seat. He had a feeling the next two days were going to be very stressful, and he needed all the rest he could get if he was going to see her safely through them.

Chapter 8

Lily was really starting to miss sleeping in a real bed. She woke up with that special stiff neck she got only from sleeping in airplane seats. Her mouth was cotton-dry, too. Dawn streaked the sky as their plane descended into Washington, D.C. The Washington Monument and the Capitol dome were awash in pink light, and a layer of haze hung low over the city.

The plane landed and taxied past the big passenger terminals to a smaller, unmarked hangar. She was startled when the plane continued right into the hangar. As its engines spooled down, the hangar doors slid shut behind them.

"Oooh, how spooky and spylike," she joked.

Carter nodded grimly. "That's the idea. Because you are, in point of fact, entering the country illegally, we thought it best to make your arrival low-key."

"Illegally?" she squeaked.

"We're going to be bypassing Customs today, which is just as well because you don't have your passport with you nor do you have any proof of where you just were."

"Couldn't you vouch for me?"

He replied, "I could, but it would take hours to go up the Customs chain of command and back down mine to sort it out. It's easier to just do it this way."

She saw the logic of it, but felt hinky breaking the law like this. The steps were duly lowered, and as she ducked out of the Learjet, Carter offered her a hand. Out of habit, she grabbed it.

So much for her never-touching-him-again promise. He'd had a pretty convincing explanation of the massacre, but she hesitated to just buy his story hook, line and sinker. She needed to think about it a little more. Listen to her gut when it decided to tell her something. Which left them in limbo.

She hated limbo. She hated both the dance of that name where drunks staggered under a pole, and she hated the state of being unsure of something and being caught in between knowing and not knowing.

A dark SUV with blacked-out windows was parked not far from the jet. Carter led her to it and she climbed into the surprisingly plush vehicle. "Nice wheels," she murmured.

The hangar doors opened enough for the SUV to drive through them, and Carter muttered back, "It's a Secret Service vehicle. Used in presidential motorcades. It's armored, and the driver is a Secret Service agent. We're not taking any chances with your safety until this thing's over."

Wow. They thought she was this important? Lily grinned. "If only Bill Kaplan could see me now. He'd have an aneurysm."

Carter gave her a small, tentative smile. "Maybe you'll be able to tell him about it someday. But truthfully, I wouldn't expect this mission to be declassified until your grandchildren are adults. And if you tell them the tale then, they'll think granny's gone off her medications again."

"I'm already batty, or so I'm told," she retorted.

"I dunno. I haven't seen any sign of it yet." Then he added drily, "But I'll let you know if I do."

"Gee, thanks."

The morning rush hour hadn't yet ground Washington traffic to a halt, and they parked underneath a snazzy hotel in northwest D.C. in about a half hour. Apparently, they'd already been checked in because Carter whisked her straight up to a room on the fourth floor.

"You want to sleep some more?" he asked. "You were pretty restless on the plane."

Something lurched inside her. He'd watched her sleep? Why would he do that? Was it just part of his job or maybe something more? Regardless, his suggestion sounded like pure heaven. She eyed the fluffy comforter and down pillows and sighed in bliss as she toppled over among them.

"Wake me up when you've saved the world," she mumbled.

He laughed quietly. "Sweet dreams, *chère.*"

Carter might have wished her sweet dreams, but his wish didn't come true. She dreamed of blood and mutilation. Of fanged children eating their mothers, and the screams of the women. And then, somehow, she was the murderer and her victim was a Russian man staring down at the gaping hole in his chest and back up at her. She glimpsed the guy's still-beating heart and jerked back violently.

"Easy, sugar. I've got you."

Lily jolted awake. Strong, warm arms held her. Her ear was pressed against Carter's chest and his heart beat slow and steady beneath it. She was safe. It was just a dream. A horrible nightmare. Not real.

What if it had been real? What if those images had been burned on her memory never to be forgotten? She might be a head case, too. Her arms crept around his waist. It wasn't fair that any human being was asked to witness such atrocities or deal directly with them. She wished fervently that all wars would end and no soldier ever had to see the things Carter had, to make the decisions he'd been forced to, done the things he'd been required to. She desperately wanted to comfort him. To cradle him in her arms and erase it all from his mind, if only for a little while.

Assuming his version of events was reasonably accurate, of course, and not a complete fabrication to assuage his guilt and trick her.

Yup, she definitely despised limbo. She couldn't bring herself to let him go, but neither could she bring herself to act upon her romantic and protective impulses. Man, this was the pits. He seemed content to just hold her, however, and she let him.

A small eternity later, she mumbled, "I suppose if I'm not going back to sleep, we might as well eat breakfast."

She thought he might have dropped a fleeting kiss in her hair before he sighed and released her. "I'll order room service. What's your pleasure?"

Her gaze snapped to his. Him? Over easy with a side of whipped cream and chocolate syrup?

Darn if his gaze didn't heat up. The man could read her like an open book.

Embarrassed that he'd caught her thinking such things about him, she belatedly replied, "A veggie omelet if they've got it. Any kind of muffin, and maybe some orange juice."

"Your wish is my command," he murmured.

Now it was her turn to feel heat in her face. The Southern boy was back to being a bit of a flirt apparently. Flustered, she retreated to the bathroom to jump into the shower. She hoped the scalding water would distract her from steamy fantasies of hunky soldiers with sexy drawls, but it didn't. Maybe there was something to the cold shower theory after all. She was too chicken to test it, however.

Carter looked up mildly from the *Washington Post* when she emerged from the bathroom. "Enjoyed your shower?" he asked.

Now why did that make her cheeks heat up? It was a simple question. Maybe it was the idea of him knowing she'd just been naked and running her soapy hands all over her body in the next room. Or maybe she was just a hot-to-trot mess.

Thankfully, breakfast arrived, and it did distract her from her errant thoughts. Particularly when Carter commented near the end of the meal, "I got a call while you were in the shower. We've got an appointment at 11:00 a.m. at the Russian Embassy."

"And we're sure no one will try to kill me the second I set foot inside there?"

"We're not sure of anything. But it's my job to keep you safe and your job to convince the ambassador that there's a serious problem with their doomsday machine."

She wasn't certain she would have any more success at doing her part of this mission than he would. But it wasn't as if they could just walk away from this crisis. They *had* to try.

"Is there any chance I can get something more… serious…to wear to this meeting?" she asked hesitantly.

"Ratty jeans and a GO ARMY sweatshirt don't exactly scream brilliant scientist."

"I dunno. You're pretty cute in that gigantic sweatshirt. It makes you look about eight years old."

"Great. Just the look I'm going for to get the Russians to take me seriously."

He leaned forward and twined his fingers with hers. "I take you pretty seriously."

Her breath hitched. That boy was going to get his bones jumped if he wasn't careful—no, wait. Strike that. There would be no bone jumping until she had more time to think. To research the truth of the Sudanese shootings.

She extracted her fingers from his gently and spoke carefully. "Let's just save the world first. Then we can figure out what comes next."

"Deal."

She frowned. He sounded entirely too pleased with that arrangement. What did he think she'd just agreed to?

"I'll call the concierge. He'll know where we can get you a nice suit fast."

A suit. Right. Save the world. "Do you suppose that if we make the world safe for humanity my university will consider that grounds to give me tenure?"

He laughed heartily. "I should think so."

She nodded resolutely. "All right, then. Let's do this."

Carter was still amused when they emerged from a women's clothing store with Lily duly attired in a charcoal-gray suit that made her look like a high-powered attorney… who was about eight years old. She was just naturally an adorable person. Those big brown eyes and innocent air about her couldn't be disguised, no matter how severe the cut of the suit.

He helped her into the double-parked SUV, which

whisked them northwest on Massachusetts Avenue toward Embassy Row. The vehicle stopped in front of the Russian Embassy's guard shack.

"Are you ready for this?" Carter asked her sotto voce.

"It's too late to back out now," she muttered back. "Ready or not, here we go."

His thighs twitched warningly. Dammit, he was more "or not" than "ready." The Secret Service driver gave the guard their names and passed their picture IDs through the window. They waited long enough that Carter's back muscles were getting into the spasming act and his shoulders were starting to feel twitchy.

"You may have to go inside without me," he ground out.

Lily's hand immediately landed on his thigh. "Oh, no, you don't. You're not making me face the big, bad wolf alone. You relax right now, mister." She started massaging him vigorously, and the tightness across his shoulders receded. As she leaned over to work on his thighs, he thanked his lucky stars that the Russians couldn't see through the windows of this vehicle.

When her hands crept higher on his legs, though, his thoughts careened off in an entirely different direction. Memory of making love to her flashed vividly through his mind's eye. Lily straddling him under the stars, moaning her pleasure to the heavens. And the damnedest thing happened. His back muscles started to unwind of their own volition.

"You may pass," the guard outside announced.

Their SUV eased forward and around the circular drive to deposit them at the front door of the large building.

"Can you walk?" Lily murmured.

He laughed painfully. "Questionable, but not because

of one of my episodes. Did you have to put your hands all over me like that?"

"Hey! I behaved."

He blinked, startled. As if she'd been considering misbehaving? She abruptly looked abashed as well. Hadn't meant to say that aloud, if he had to guess. "Now we really have to save the world. I want to see exactly what you were really imagining."

Her cheeks pinkened as he opened the door and he made a careful visual sweep of the area. He spied no threats to her, but he doubted that he'd spot a sniper here if there were one. After all, he didn't see any cameras, but he knew without a shadow of a doubt they were here, too.

Carter held out a hand to help her out of the car, and she grabbed the folder of printouts of the simulation data and joined him under the covered porch. He tried to stand close enough to provide cover for her, but not so close as to look like he was crowding her, or worse, hovering protectively. They couldn't afford to insult the Russians at this juncture by acting like they thought the Russians were going to shoot them—even if that was exactly what he thought.

"Shall we?" he said much more casually than he felt.

"We shall," she said firmly.

Yup, courageous woman.

He wasn't surprised when they were forced to sit on low, uncomfortable sofas and wait for nearly a half hour for their meeting. It was a standard Russian negotiating strategy to throw an opponent off balance by making them feel ill at ease and impatient. To her credit, Lily didn't fidget or seem flapped in the least. Maybe lack of punctuality was commonplace in academia.

Finally, an attractive secretary led them into a sitting room decorated in the Imperial style. Another standard Russian tactic. Make the opponent feel inferior and overwhelmed by Russian wealth and might. Lily, bless her, merely commenced circling the room and inspecting various works of art with interest. She didn't seem the slightest bit overwhelmed.

They waited some more, which seemed just fine with Lily, who was having a ball exploring the room's treasures. For his part, he sat back and enjoyed watching her. He never got tired of looking at her beauty. She almost didn't seem real sometimes. It was as if a fairy had tried to take human form and not quite got it right. An ethereal, otherworldly quality clung to her.

The door burst open and a large man in a Russian Army uniform strode into the room. Carter rose to his feet slowly enough to signal that he wasn't intimidated.

"Welcome, welcome," the man said loudly. "How may I help you today?"

The guy seemed friendly enough, but Carter wasn't fooled for a second. He replied, "We have an appointment with the ambassador this morning."

"I'm so sorry. He is not available today. Important affairs of state come up, you know."

Lily startled Carter by interjecting smoothly, "Yes, we know. In fact, we're here to discuss a most important affair of state with him ourselves. We'll be happy to wait until he has a free moment."

Carter suppressed a grin as consternation flashed across the Russian's face. But then the man's gaze hardened. "The ambassador will not be available at all today. You must speak to me."

Lily shrugged and looked the guy up and down, completely unimpressed with his medals and insignia of rank. For his part, Carter had already identified the man as a highly decorated Spetsnaz officer—Russian Special Forces—a man not to be taken lightly.

Lily asked bluntly, "Who are you?" The Russian blinked, startled as she barged on without giving him time to answer. "Mind you, I don't need to know your name. I'm sure I couldn't pronounce it or your rank without butchering them, so I won't try. What I mean is, do you have high enough security clearances to hear what we're here to talk about? I'll need to see something in writing before I speak with you."

Carter had to work not to burst out laughing. The Russian was stunned speechless that some slip of an American girl was not only questioning his security clearances, but demanding proof of them.

"I am senior military attaché to United States, missy," the Russian spluttered, his accent noticeably thicker.

Carter grinned. Damn, she was good. She had the guy completely off balance. Taking pity on the man, he intervened. "Lily, this gentleman is, indeed, the attaché here. I recognize his face. He'll have a high enough clearance to hear about your findings…" he paused for effect "…barely."

The Russian puffed up like a rooster and actually strutted a lap around the room while trying to regain his composure. Lily moved over to the sofa, sat down and leaned back calmly to wait the man out. Carter was amazed. Where had she learned how to handle men like this?

Finally, the Russian sank down on the sofa facing them.

"Now, then," Lily started briskly. "I'm an astrophysicist, and I've made a discovery that not only affects our two countries, but also the entire world."

The Russian's bushy eyebrows climbed his forehead a fraction.

"It turns out a small, insignificant asteroid is going to

strike a deserted region of Siberia in approximately one week."

The Russian shrugged. "Meteors. Asteroids. They hit Earth every day."

"True," Lily replied serenely, "but they don't hit at the exact location of your country's doomsday machine. And this one's going to."

"Doomsday…what…we have no…impossible…" the man spluttered.

Carter honestly didn't get a read on whether the man knew about the machine or not. Either way, the Russian's shock was genuine as Lily went on to briefly outline the forecasted impact, shock wave, EMP pulse and crater damage, and then to state that those met all the parameters to force an automatic detonation of Russia's entire nuclear arsenal by the doomsday system, the existence of which he was so busily wasting his breath pretending wasn't real.

"You have proof?" the Russian finally blurted.

"Of course." She laid a copy of her calculations on top of the photograph of the asteroid. "The math is complicated, but our scientists have verified all of it."

The Russian took one look at the strings of letter and figures inside the file and bolted to his feet. "This is madness. Although, I shall, of course, take all precautions and send your math to the university to be checked."

Lily, in turn, leaped to her feet. "There's no time for that! Didn't you hear me? The asteroid's going to hit in a matter of days. And your country's going to accidentally destroy the world if you don't disable your machine before the impact."

Unfortunately, the attaché chose that particular moment to regain his mental footing. He blustered, "I categorically deny that my country has any such device."

Carter leaned back, thinking fast. That sounded true. It was completely possible that this guy had never heard of the doomsday machine. Attachés the world over were thinly veiled official spies. At the end of the day, this guy was a flunky in the Russian power structure and not even that high-ranking.

Carter intervened gently, "I realize, sir, that your important duties here may keep you too busy to get briefed on obscure defense systems your country maintains in central Siberia. But this asteroid is all too real, and it's going to land very soon. If such a hypothetical doomsday device did exist, it would be extremely important for officials at the very highest levels of your government to make sure such a device were turned off and left off until after this asteroid has landed."

The Russian's gaze narrowed. He was being massaged. He knew it and clearly didn't like it. Would he tell the ambassador about this? Or maybe run it up the Russian military chain of command instead? Carter couldn't tell. The man was too good at masking his intentions.

"My secretary will show you out," the Russian announced stiffly. He pressed a button on the wall, and the doors opened immediately. The secretary from before stood there.

Carter paused in the act of passing by the man and murmured in his fluent Russian, "From one special operator to another, we're telling you the God's honest truth. You have my word on it. Do what you have to, comrade, to get someone to listen to you."

It was all he could do. Carter took Lily's arm and escorted her from the building. They climbed into the SUV and had no sooner cleared the gates than his cell phone rang. He should've known. H.O.T. Watch had been watching them from above the whole time.

Brady Hathaway spoke tersely in his ear. "Did the ambassador buy it?"

"We didn't get to speak with him. We got passed off to an attaché. And I have no idea whether or not he believed us. He seemed to genuinely believe that no doomsday machine exists."

"For everyone's sake, I hope he's right," Brady replied grimly. "But our intelligence sources on the subject are impeccable. It exists, all right."

Carter sighed. "I don't know if our attaché will stick his neck out and risk his career by running this information up the chain of command or not. Frankly, he didn't strike me as the type."

Brady responded, "We'll watch the message traffic for the next few hours to see if we can get a read on it."

"Any instructions for us?"

"Get our girl under cover and stand by for further instructions."

Carter's lips twitched. He'd love nothing better than to get under the covers with Lily. "Yes, sir. Understood."

They headed back to the hotel and were in time to catch the noon news. It seemed anticlimactic after all the drama of the past few days.

"Is that it?" Lily asked. "Is it over?"

Carter sighed. "Do you think he believed us?"

"I think he believes an asteroid's going to hit Siberia. I don't think he believes the doomsday machine exists."

"That's how I read him, too. And that being the case, I expect we're not done talking to folks about this problem."

"Well, at least the Russians know now they didn't stop

me from giving you all my research. They don't have to kill me anymore."

Carter didn't disabuse her of the optimistic thought. Personally, his fear was that now the Russians would decide that, instead of just her having to die, both of them had to die.

Chapter 9

Lily paced the confines of the hotel room, agitated. Carter insisted on keeping the heavy curtains closed for security reasons. She understood why, but her dratted claustrophobia was starting to kick in again.

"We've got a problem," she finally announced.

"What's that?" Carter looked up from a news program on the television.

"The walls are closing in on me."

"I'm fairly sure they're not moving. I hear they squeak and groan terribly when they close in and crush someone. And then, of course, there's all the screaming and bones crunching."

"Very funny." She scowled at him.

"What can I do to help?" he asked more seriously.

She planted her hands on her hips. "You do realize that we're standing at ground zero of a nuclear attack on the United States by Russia."

"Yes. And?"

"And if we fail to convince someone to listen to us, we'll be crispy critters by this time next week. It could all be over in an instant."

"It's been that way for the past sixty years, and we're still standing here talking about it."

"Be serious, Carter. We could be living our last days on Earth."

He crossed his arms and contemplated her soberly. "This is just now occurring to you?"

"I've been too busy trying to run around with you and stay alive, not to mention trying to figure out if my calculations could be wrong, to stop and think about it until now."

"Welcome to my world. Threats to the continued survival of mankind have cropped up from time to time before. It's just that the general public never hears about them. Well, except for the Bay of Pigs incident. We got within about ten minutes of nuclear war on that one. Thing is, we've always managed to come through the crises. We'll make it through this one, too."

"I thought I was the incurable optimist and you were the big pessimist."

He shrugged.

She wrung her hands and stared at the walls which, despite his quips, were definitely shrinking in on her inch by inch. "I've got to get out of here."

"No can do, sugar."

"Why not?"

"I'm under orders to keep you safe and under cover."

Her gaze snapped to his. Did he intend the double entendre?

He smiled wryly, but his eyes remained grim. What was

that about? Something was wrong. Something he wasn't telling her. Something that had him big-time worried.

"Talk to me, Carter. What are you thinking?"

"I'm thinking that I'd do just about anything to get you under the covers, but I can't. You'd be mad at yourself for doing it, and I'd be mad at myself for seducing you."

"But what if I wanted you to seduce me?"

"You'd want me to distract you. That's entirely different."

"Well, I'm here to tell you a game of cards or a pay-per-view movie isn't going to do the trick," she declared.

"You've obviously never played strip poker," he retorted.

Her gaze narrowed. "Big words from a man who's not prepared to follow through on them."

He smiled. "You know, if I were a less mature person, I'd feel obliged to pick up that gauntlet you just threw down. But I happen to know better. Sorry."

Damn, damn, damn! "Carter, you've got to get me out of here."

"It's not safe."

"What if we wear disguises?"

"Better, but still stupid."

"What if we only go downstairs and take a peek in the shops in that arcade off the hotel lobby?" When he didn't answer right away, she added, "Pleeeease?"

He gave her a regretful look.

She spoke quickly before he could say no. "Look, I've done everything you people have asked without complaint. I've run all over creation. I've left my home and my job, and God knows if I'll ever get tenure now. I haven't complained when people kept trying to kill me. Heck, I even shot a man. I've let you take me and my claustrophobia into salt mines and mini-subs and hollow mountains without making too big a fuss about it. All I'm asking is to get out of this room for a little while. The world may be coming to an end, and I just want to go downstairs and have a look around. Is that too much to ask?"

His mouth twitched. "Let me get this straight. The world is about to end, so you want to get in a little last-minute shopping?"

Oh, God. He was right. If her parents ever found out how she'd caved to petty materialism in the end, they'd be mortified. "Well, yes," she answered defensively.

Carter started to chuckle. It became a laugh, and then a shout of humor.

"It's not that funny," she declared.

"Oh, yes, it is," he gasped. "You've just proven that at your cores, all women are the same. I get it now. I can die a happy man. I finally unraveled the mystery of the female mind."

"Not all women like shopping, you know," she snapped.

The comment sent him off into renewed gales of laughter. She gave up on the argument and just rolled her eyes until his amusement finally subsided.

"Okay, fine. You win," he announced. She listened as he called the concierge and asked for a woman's blond wig to be sent upstairs.

He got off the phone and she demanded, "And you think the hotel's just going to have something like that lying around waiting for a guest to request?" she demanded.

Carter grinned. "This hotel is infamous as the place high rollers bring their mistresses and…professional dates. They'll have a wig."

"Hmm. And you say women are all the same. Men are *definitely* all the same. They think about one thing and one thing only."

"Oh, like women don't think about sex all the time, too?"

She pounced. "Then you don't deny that men do it?"

"Of course I don't deny it," he said blandly.

He took all the fun out of winning an argument. Lily did her best not to pout until the wig did indeed arrive a few minutes later. She retreated to the bathroom, where she tucked her long, dark hair up under the short wig. She went heavy with her makeup and suddenly looked like an entirely different person. In short, she looked like a slut. It was kind of fun actually. She was glad she got to dress up like this once before she died.

Died. And all of a sudden, she was breathing hard, the tiny bathroom squeezing all the air out of her lungs. She tore open the door and burst out into the main room.

Carter whirled around, alarmed. But then he just stared. "Lily?" he asked.

"Who else would it be?" she retorted.

"You don't think maybe you should be a little less conspicuous for this outing of ours?"

She grinned. "So what if I draw attention? No one will recognize me."

"I should say not." He cleared his throat uncomfortably.

She wagged a finger at him. "Don't you dare tell me that the whole men prefer blondes thing is true. I have a week left to live. Let me keep my delusions that some men like brunettes."

"Hey, most men just want their women breathing. They're not too much pickier than that."

"Sex freaks, all of you."

"Says the pot to the kettle," he shot back. He pulled a baseball cap low on his forehead, casting his face into shadows. He'd turned the GO ARMY sweatshirt inside out and cut off its sleeves while she was in the bathroom. And as a disguise, she had to admit it was effective. She had a hard time looking away from his impressively bulging biceps long enough to register anything about his shadow-obscured face.

The mini-mall next to the hotel's lobby wasn't crowded, but Lily had the right of it. The few women there were riveted by the sight of Carter's arms. Every few minutes some new female would spy him, and Lily cracked up to watch them gape. For her part, she had a ball sashaying down the broad arcade, swinging her hips at every man there.

"You're enjoying looking like a hooker, aren't you?" Carter murmured to her.

"Absolutely."

"Fine. Just don't look at any of those other guys. I'd hate to have to break their jaws."

"Ah, the Neanderthal within emerges."

"Damn straight, woman."

Carter's irritation sent her into gales of laughter. Who'd have guessed that facing the extinction of mankind could be so liberating?

But then Carter swore quietly under his breath, and in an instant, all humor evaporated between them. "The Russians are here. I don't think they've seen us. Yet." He took her elbow and steered her back toward the lobby quickly. But it wasn't quick enough for him. She felt him stumble. Start to move stiffly. Crud. He couldn't freeze up now!

"Go to our room," he bit out. "I'll lead them away from you."

"Not happening, big guy," she bit back.

He scowled, but rather than argue, he ducked into the nearest store and headed fast for the back and its dressing rooms. He shoved her inside the first one and pulled the door shut behind them.

They waited for several tense, endless minutes, but no one burst in on them.

Eventually he muttered under his breath, "Did you happen to notice what kind of store this is?"

She glanced up at the garments scattered on hangers around the space. Oh, my. It was all lingerie. Sexy, naughty lingerie. The kind call girls and mistresses—or at least their male clients—were apparently fond of.

She made the mistake of glancing up into Carter's eyes. "Any port in a storm, eh?" she choked out.

He laughed silently, his entire body shaking with it. He was definitely not freezing up this time.

"I do believe you're getting better," she declared.

Surprise lit his face.

"You may be right. If nothing else, no one has ever managed to make me laugh when I'm about to die."

She looked down, abashed. How cool would that be if she had some kind of special connection with him? *Hello... you're still in limbo,* a voice reminded her in the back of her head.

Screw limbo. If she was about to die, she shouldn't stand on principle with this totally hot man. She'd already caved to crass materialism in the face of possible annihilation. What did it matter if she turned out to be wanton hedonist, too?

Thing was, Carter's story about the massacre rang true. He didn't strike her as the kind of person who could even contemplate harming innocent children. If he said they'd had guns and been on the verge of killing him and his men, she was inclined to believe him.

Of course, maybe that was just her lust and wishful thinking talking. Maybe she so desperately wanted to believe him because she so badly didn't want him to be a monster. Call her naive, call her willfully ignorant. But she didn't want to live in a world where massacres like the reporter had described were real.

"Carter," she murmured, "do you think anyone saw us come in here?"

"They'd have broken down the door or just shot us through it by now if they had."

"So, then, we're alone?"

"I don't see anyone else."

She rolled her eyes. He was totally missing the broad hints she was throwing at him. Apparently, she was going to have to show him exactly what she was thinking about.

She stretched up on her tiptoes and pressed herself against him pretty much from neck to toes. He took a sharp breath and the light dawned in his gaze. Neanderthal was becoming clever Homo sapien before her very eyes. She whispered, "If this were your last day on Earth, what would you do with it?"

He caught that hint, thank goodness.

His arms swept around her and he dragged her up against him until her feet barely touched the floor. "You're sure about this?"

She laughed. "I thought you'd never get around to it."

As his mouth closed over hers, he turned, pressing her back against the wall, thrusting his thigh forward until she rode upon it, rubbing the most sensitive parts of her against his hard muscles in a tantalizing dance. His hand moved between them and her skirt fell away from her heated flesh. And then his fingers were upon her, stroking and teasing while he murmured endearments. The blouse fell away next and then her bra.

Carter turned her to face the mirror, her back pressed against him. She was stunned to see herself in the floor-length mirror, a naked, sexy blonde twisting in the arms of a fully clothed man like some sort of sex goddess. The sight was impossibly erotic. His hands, big and tanned, moved all over her pale slender body, possessing her, marking her. And everywhere they went she burned for him.

She arched into his touch, begging throatily for more and groaning her pleasure when he gave her what she asked for. He wove a magic spell around her that made her vision blur at the edges and colored lights sparkle in her eyes. And then he was inside her, thrusting hot steel into her swollen, velvet flesh.

She'd have cried out if his finger hadn't been in her mouth, thrusting in and out in erotic imitation of the other act. She sucked his finger, drawing it into the wet depths of her mouth, milking it with tongue and teeth, licking and stroking as his tempo increased in speed and power. Again and again, he plunged into her and she pushed back, reveling in being taken so completely.

It started as a tingling in her fingers and toes and built in scope, traveling down her limbs toward her core, growing like a tsunami as it raced ashore. And as Carter touched the very core of her, the wave broke, crashing over her, submerging her and finally drowning her. Their bodies shuddered violently together until slowly, slowly, the tension drained from them both.

He sank down to the bench, cradling her in his arms until she regained the ability to think and speak.

"Feeling better about the end of the world?" he murmured.

Lily laughed ruefully. "I am feeling better. Maybe not about the whole dying-horribly-at-any-moment bit, though."

"You get used to it after a while."

She laid her head on his shoulder. "I don't think I'll ever get used to this," she confessed.

His arms tightened around her, but he made no reply.

Eventually, she asked, "What are you thinking about?"

"I think I like the red lace teddy more than that black leather bustier."

She lurched and looked up at the hangers on the wall left over from a previous customer. "You're incorrigible."

"Guilty as charged. Do you need help, uh, putting yourself back together?"

She pulled on her clothes and retucked her hair up under the wig. But her makeup was hopelessly smeared and she ended up taking most of it off with a tissue she dug out of her purse.

Carter insisted on opening the door and leaving first, so she only heard the pert voice of the sales girl asking him archly, "Did you find something you liked?"

Lily gritted her teeth in humiliation as Carter laughed knowingly. "Why, yes, I did. I'll take the blonde—oh, and the red teddy."

Hastily, Lily snatched up the barely there teddy and followed him to the cash register. He paid for the purchase and handed her the discreet bag while she fumed behind him.

When their hotel-room door finally closed behind them, she turned on him accusingly. "You let that girl think I'm a hooker!"

"What do you care? We'll all be dead in a week. Live in the moment, kid. It's the trick to true happiness."

"How can you talk so casually about Armageddon?" she demanded, irritated.

He sat down on the edge of the bed and looked at her intently. "I'm not kidding. None of us have any way of knowing when our number will be up. You or I could be hit by a car while crossing the street tomorrow and never live to see the end of the world next week. Life isn't a certain thing. The only thing any of us can do is find everything we can to appreciate what's right around us and enjoy what we can in this exact moment."

She sat down beside him and stared back at him.

He continued, "If you want to get philosophical about it, neither the past nor the future actually exists. We only have memory of one and anticipation of what the other might be like. All that ever truly exists is the now."

"But we have the results of the past to live with, and we can shape the future with our decisions now."

"True. I'm not saying we should ignore the past and future. I'm just saying it's vital to notice the now. To experience it. To really *live* each moment—not just float along waiting for some future moment to occur or wishing for some moment that's already gone."

Frankly, she was shocked. Who'd have guessed a soldier would take such an existential view of life? Darned if the man wasn't even more attractive when he was being all intelligent and thoughtful.

"What's wrong?" he asked suddenly. "Why are you looking at me with pity like that?"

"I was just thinking what a tragedy it is that men have such long recovery times between sexual encounters while we women don't."

"Uh-ho. Now those are fighting words, madam."

She blinked at him, startled. Without warning he tipped her over on her back and pounced. "Guess we're not going to get to try out the sexy lingerie this time either," he murmured against her stomach as he shoved her blouse out of the way again. "Recovery time. Ha!"

Well, all right, then. Apparently, her hypothesis that men wanted sex only every few days or at most, once a day, was mistaken. In fact, over the next few hours, Carter showed her exactly how wildly mistaken she'd been.

His life-changing demonstration was only ended when his cell phone rang on the bedside table. Emerging from under the covers, his hair sticking up every which way and a wide grin on his face as she swore at the interruption, he reached across her for the device.

"Baigneaux here. Go." A pause. "Hi, boss."

Carter listened intently for several agonizingly long and silent moments. And then he only said, "Wilco," before disconnecting the call.

"Well?" she demanded as he set the phone down again.

"I thought you were mad at the interruption," he said innocently.

She tugged on his hair to keep him from disappearing beneath the sheets again. "Okay, fine. So women are insatiably curious. I admit it."

"When they're not shopping, that is."

Laughing, she punched his shoulder lightly. "C'mon. Spill the beans."

"H.O.T. Watch has arranged some time on the Hubble for you this evening. You're going to get that closer look at your asteroid that you need to verify its mass and velocity exactly. We need a precise impact date and time."

"When?" she asked eagerly.

"We don't have to leave for a couple of hours. Long enough for me to prove to you once and for all that the hyperorgasmic cluster is no myth at all."

Oh, my. She could get used to his brand of science. Very used to it, indeed.

Chapter 10

It took them nearly an hour to reach the NASA Goddard facility in the Maryland suburbs of Washington, D.C., in their armored SUV. Plenty of time for Carter to wonder what the hell had happened to change Lily's mind about him. Or maybe her mind hadn't changed at all. Maybe she still thought he was a baby killer and murderer of the worst sort. Maybe none of that mattered in the face of Armageddon. Maybe it all came down to him simply being the closest available male when the world was about to end.

Thing was, she was so much more than merely the nearest convenient female for him. He'd been so damned proud of how she'd handled herself at the Russian Embassy. Not to mention she was having the darnedest effect on his freeze-ups. It was as if all the laughter she brought to his life was healing him. Either that or the great sex. She was brave and unconcerned for her own safety, and he couldn't help but admire those traits in her, no matter how misplaced they might be from time to time. And in their hotel room this afternoon…she was one hell of a woman and not afraid to show it. How could he not fall for her? She was everything he'd ever dreamed of and more.

Women all over the world must be laughing tonight that the tables had finally been turned on the ever-charming and ever-elusive Carter Baigneaux. He'd always been the one to leave them pining for him as he moved on to the next hot spot, the next crisis. But would Lily leave him behind if—when, dammit—this one was successfully resolved? God, he hated not knowing.

Getting through the various layers of security at the Goddard facility took a while, and he was blessedly distracted by all the rigmarole. They were finally escorted to the main communications center, which looked like a miniature version of Houston's massive control room.

An engineer explained that the Hubble was currently on the far side of Earth, and tonight, its information would be relayed to Washington via the International Space Station. Lily nodded, concentrating intently on what everyone told her. Darned if he wasn't turned on by her display of formidable intelligence as she questioned the scientists around her about the Hubble's capabilities to image the asteroid and succinctly listed exactly what information she required.

Work, Boudreau. Work. Save the world now. Seduce the girl after.

The asteroid's estimated coordinates were duly fed to the Hubble, and the space-based telescope began a ponderous turn toward the region of the galaxy from which death hurtled at them all. Lily fidgeted beside him until Carter surreptitiously took her hand in his.

"Nervous?" he murmured.

"Excited. This is every astronomer's dream—to have one of the greatest telescopes ever created at her personal beck and call."

He was glad to have made a dream come true for her in case things turned out badly. Good Lord willing, he'd make at least a few more of her dreams come true before the end. Boy, was he becoming a sap! What *had* that woman done to him?

"Here it comes," she said eagerly. Every eye in the room turned to the big screen, where a fuzzy image was slowly coming into focus of a pitted chunk of gray rock. "That picture's amazing!" she exclaimed.

"You said you need spectroscopy of the object to determine its mineral content?" one of the engineers asked.

"Yes. In particular, we need to know its exact density, mass and velocity."

"The scan will take several minutes," the engineer replied, already typing into his computer. "It's a lot like an MRI—we'll scan the asteroid in slices and then compile a composite image."

About halfway through the slices stacking up on the screens before them, a loud voice startled everyone in the facility. "Goddard, this is Mir. Acknowledge." *Mir* was the Russian word for *peace*. It was also the name of the International Space Station.

Crap. That voice had a distinct Russian accent.

"Go ahead, Mir," the duty controller replied.

"We see you make unscheduled move with Hubble. For why you deviate from schedule?"

The controller looked over at Carter for guidance. Carter asked quietly, "Can Mir hear us right now?"

"No, sir. I've got us off speaker."

"This is a highly classified situation. We can't tell the Russians what we're doing—"

"Why not?" Lily interrupted.

Carter turned to her. "This is a military crisis. We can't just share that with everyone who happens to be Russian. We don't want to create a global panic."

"Yes, but this is a cosmonaut. He won't randomly panic," she said urgently. "What if we tell him exactly what we're looking at? What if we make it crystal clear that this is incredibly urgent and important? Won't he report that to his superiors right away? And won't a bunch of Russians very highly placed in their space program start asking questions about why the Americans are so frantically looking at some insignificant little asteroid that's about to slam into Siberia?"

"It's totally against protocol," he replied doubtfully.

"Protocol, schmotocol. We're all going to die anyway."

Gasps around the room greeted that announcement. Damn. He was going to have to make everyone here sign security statements before they left.

"Fine," he bit out. He turned to the duty controller. "Tell the cosmonaut exactly what we're pointing the Hubble at and that it's a matter of highest and most urgent U.S. national security."

The controller nodded and relayed the message. A long, long silence was Mir's only reply.

"Ten to one he's on the horn to the Russian Space Agency this very second," Lily muttered.

"I wouldn't take that bet," Carter murmured back. "You'd win."

Finally, the Russian's scratchy voice filled the room once more. "Say why small asteroid is emergency, Goddard."

Carter looked up at Lily. They made eye contact and understanding flowed between them. This was an all-or-nothing situation. The same kind he'd faced in the Sudan, and the same kind she'd faced up on that bluff.

He leaned forward and punched the transmit button on the comm panel. "Do me a favor, Mir. Ask your superiors to turn off the doomsday machine located at ground zero where this asteroid is projected to impact Earth. On behalf of mankind, we would all love to live out the week."

"Uh, roger, Goddard. Copy."

"What the hell's going on, Captain?" the senior controller demanded. "What's this about doomsday?"

Carter sighed. "I've just breached every security procedure ever enacted by our country. I really can't say any more. In fact, when the dust settles from this whole mess, assuming any of us are still alive, there's probably going to be a hell of a stink about what I just did. You might want to just arrest me now to cover your behind."

The guy frowned, thought for a minute. "Is there more you two can do to prevent this doomsday thing?"

"Maybe."

The man looked around the control center, making eye contact with each of his people. "Then I'm pretty sure I didn't hear anything at all about any doomsday device. I was asked to relay some data on a chunk of rock to some scientist, and that's what I did."

There were nods all around.

Carter nodded back gratefully at the man.

"Carter?" It was Lily, speaking from the computer she'd sat down at the minute the cross sections of the asteroid were complete. And she was as white as a sheet.

"What've you got?"

"We've got a problem. A huge one. Our asteroid is, indeed, comprised totally of heavy metals."

"Which means?" he asked.

"We're not looking at a week. We're looking at more like two days."

He gasped, appalled. Finally, he cleared his throat and ordered, "Print it all in hard copy and then save it to the flash drive."

She got to work. While she did, the controller sidled up to him. "Is there anything we can do to help?"

"Yeah. Say a prayer when you go to bed tonight that saner heads prevail. And hug your kids."

"Amen," the guy murmured.

"Okay, I've got it." Lily brandished a sheaf of papers.

"Thank you for your help, gentlemen," Carter said to the room in general. "Let's go, Lily. We've got a world to save."

He herded her into the SUV and told the driver to take them back to the hotel.

"Now what?" she asked him.

"Now it's time for H.O.T. Watch to call in the big guns." He pulled out his phone and reported the revised impact date grimly to Brady and what they'd said to the Russian cosmonaut. Lily was watching impatiently when he disconnected the call. "Brady says to get some rest while they make some calls. This could take a while. It's getting late and people can be hard to reach at this hour."

"Rest?" she exclaimed. "He's joking, right?"

"No, he's not. And he's right. We have no idea what tomorrow will bring. Best to sleep now while we can. We may not get another chance." *Ever.* Cripes. That was a sobering thought. He might never sleep again after tonight. Might never lie down with Lily and make love to her again. He wasn't prone to wallowing in maudlin emotions, but the notion was enough to choke a guy up a little.

"You okay?" Lily murmured. "You're going tense."

"I was just thinking about how I like being alive."

"Me, too."

The rest of the ride back to the hotel passed in silence. They made love slowly and sweetly and cuddled in the dark together for a long time afterward. Although they didn't speak, he could tell from her breathing that she wasn't asleep either. Being this close to the end of everything sure put a man's life in perspective. He didn't think about career accomplishments or stuff he'd like to have owned. He thought about his family. Friends he'd like to see one more time so he could tell them how much they'd meant to him. About the kids he might have had. How much he'd have enjoyed having Lily for his wife.

After a while, she reached up and flicked at her cheek like she was dashing a tear away.

"I know the feeling," he said quietly.

"This sucks," she mumbled.

"Tomorrow morning, call your parents. It'll make you feel better."

She half laughed, half sobbed, "What would really make me feel better would be to call Bill Kaplan and tell him to go suck an egg."

"Then by all means do that, too. We'll both make some calls tomorrow."

She nodded against his shoulder. It wasn't long after that she drifted to sleep. At least one of them was getting a little rest. But then, she probably had a clear conscience about her life. He had a whole lot of faces in his noggin. Faces of the children he'd killed. Children he had a reckoning with. Soon.

Lily was subdued when she woke up the next morning. She couldn't believe she'd actually slept. It must be some sort of defense mechanism of the human mind to put a person to sleep when the reality around them became too much to stand.

She and Carter both made a bunch of phone calls first thing. Odd, awkward conversations to tell people how much they missed them and cared about them, and of course, calls to family to say "I love you." Just in case, of course.

Both of them were quiet over a late breakfast.

He'd pushed the food cart out into the hall and came back before she asked, "No word from H.O.T. Watch yet?"

It was as if she'd conjured the phone call, for at that moment, his cell phone rang. He pulled it out and shoved it to his ear. "Go," he said tersely.

She felt it in his sudden tension. An electricity hovering about him. They'd been given something to do. The waiting was over. Thank God.

"What's the plan?" she demanded eagerly.

"We're taking a little road trip."

"Where to?"

"Camp David."

"Isn't that where the president hangs out?" she blurted.

"One and the same."

Whoa. "Who are we going to talk to?"

"Apparently, the cabinet's having a little retreat up there with the president this weekend. I don't know who we'll talk to once we get there. Brady just said to take the SUV and get up there."

Packing was an easy matter. Her new suit fit in a single shopping bag along with the things Jennifer Blackfoot had given her a lifetime ago at H.O.T. Watch headquarters. And the red teddy…well, it fit in her pocket.

Their driver grunted in surprise when Carter told him where they were going but dutifully pointed the vehicle northwest out of town without any further comment. Lily sat back to watch the rolling Maryland countryside go past the window. She was surprised at how quickly the D.C. suburbs transitioned to fields and pastures and stands of trees—quintessential America. She desperately hoped all this bucolic beauty was still here at this time tomorrow.

Twenty-five hours and counting.

They'd been driving for maybe an hour when she spotted something diving and swooping outside, swallow-like, yet too big and fast to be a bird. "What's that?" she asked.

Carter looked where she pointed. "Crop duster."

"That looks dangerous. He's coming so close to the trees."

"It is dangerous. Those guys are a little bit crazy. Look, he's coming this way. If you stick that red teddy out the window and wave it at him, I bet he'll buzz the car."

"Carter!"

He grinned at her.

The plane was indeed coming straight at them. Maybe a hundred yards from the highway, the bright yellow plane veered hard to its left and swooped up into the sky out of sight from inside the vehicle.

But then, without warning, a mighty roar of sound blasted overhead, and the crop duster filled their windshield entirely in shocking yellow paint. He couldn't be more than ten feet above the SUV. And then a cloud of white spray completely covered the windshield.

"The bastard just sprayed us!" the driver shouted, slamming on the brakes. Carter barely heard the guy through the glass partition. Carter glanced back over his shoulder. There was no other vehicle anywhere close to them. A frisson of alarm skated up his spine.

"What the—" the driver slurred. The SUV swerved violently, and the guy slumped over the wheel all of a sudden. White foam spurted from his mouth.

"What's happening?" Lily cried.

"Brace yourself!" Carter shouted.

The SUV skidded off the highway, slammed head-first into a ditch and then rolled over violently twice. Carter hit his head on the window and saw stars, but grabbed frantically at the door. "Get outside!" he hollered.

He tore at the door handle, but it didn't release. Punching at the window button, he nearly cried in relief as the bulletproof glass panel slid down about three-quarters of the way. He grabbed Lily's arm and yanked her toward him.

She was conscious, but disoriented and dazed. He didn't feel much better. The vehicle was upside down, but she'd managed to release her seat belt and tumble in an awkward pile to the roof of the SUV.

"Take a deep breath, *chère,* and don't let it out until I tell you, okay?" She nodded fuzzily but obediently took a deep breath and held it. He did the same. Whatever that crop duster had sprayed on the car had taken out the driver in a matter of seconds. His guess was nerve gas. Sarin, maybe. Had the glass privacy panel not been raised, they'd both be dead already.

He crawled out the window, never letting go of Lily and forcing her to crawl out after him. They were in about six inches of muddy water, and the cold of it seemed to shock her to fuller consciousness. His lungs burned with the need to breathe, but grimly, he held his breath. He dragged her up and out of the ditch and blessedly felt a breeze on his skin. He turned until they faced upwind of the SUV.

"Okay, you can breathe," he told Lily.

She exhaled gustily. "What happened?"

"I think someone just made a darned good attempt to kill us." He heard an airplane engine droning in the distance and he swore violently. They needed cover. Now! The nearest tree was all the way across a large field.

He talked fast. "We've got to hide from that crop duster. I think he sprayed a nerve agent at us. Deadly gas may be collecting down in that ditch. We have to hold our breaths and go back down there and use the SUV for cover until he passes. Can you do that? It's absolutely vital that you not breathe."

She nodded. "I understand."

They both took several deep breaths as a yellow speck came into sight in the distance. It grew larger rapidly.

"Let's go." He took one last deep breath and rushed down the steep bank to the front end of the SUV. He scrambled under the engine block, which upside down, made a nice overhang for them to hide under.

Lily joined him, but then lurched hard against him. He glanced over at her. Oh, Lord. The driver, clearly dead, his face frozen in an agonized rictus of terror and pain, was crumpled against the windshield no more than a foot from her face. Carter grabbed her and pulled her face down against his shoulder.

The drone of the airplane drew closer. Closer. And then with a deafening whine, it shot past them. He scrambled out of the ditch once more, dragging Lily with him. They both panted, catching their breath as the plane arced off to the west and disappeared into the distance.

"I don't think he'll be back," Carter said quietly.

"Who was that?" she asked.

"My guess is Russian Army. Spetsnaz, probably."

"What? Why?"

He answered grimly, "I'd lay odds the attaché we spoke to yesterday didn't go to the Russian ambassador. Instead, he took your information and ran it up the Russian military chain of command. They're freaking out that the Americans know about their nasty little secret in Siberia, and they're desperate to keep you and me from telling anyone about it. Notice that this attack was definitely designed to kill, and was targeted at both of us this time and not just you. I'd say you and I just vaulted to the very top of the Russian Army's most wanted list."

"Great. Now what?"

He looked around. There wasn't a house in sight, and not another car in either direction. "We keep moving. For all we know, the Russians have a team in the area prepared to move in and confirm the kill. We've got to get out of here."

"Seriously? You think they're that determined to get us dead?"

He took off hiking down one of the rows of tender corn plants in the field. "They just attacked us with an airplane full of what was probably highly illegal and difficult-to-manufacture-and-store nerve gas. That pilot had to be wearing a full chemical warfare suit or he'd be dead, too. They knew where we were going. What route we took. What car we were in. When we'd be passing by here. Do you have any idea the amount of coordination and resources this hit took? And the Russians pulled it together in under twenty-four hours. Speaking from an operational perspective, it's as impressive as hell."

She stumbled along behind him, her jaw agape. "This isn't happening. I'm dreaming."

"I wish you were, sugar. But this is entirely real. Can you go faster? I want to get under those trees as soon as possible."

"Are you going to call H.O.T. Watch?" she panted, hustling along behind him in the soft dirt.

"As soon as we're under cover." And then he was going to pray. Hard.

Chapter 11

She must be dazed from the accident because Lily was having a hard time wrapping her brain around the fact that someone had just sprayed poison at them and nearly killed them. Had the driver's reflexes not been so fast and had he not slowed the vehicle down so much before he died and lost control of the SUV, the crash alone could have killed them.

Carter put on a last burst of speed that nearly left her in the dust of the cornfield, but she forced her tired legs to go just a few more steps. Thankfully, he stopped as soon as they reached the shade of a long row of trees.

"Get down," he ordered. "These blackberries are scratchy, but they provide decent cover."

She didn't care if the bushes had knife blades growing on them. She plunked down next to Carter on her rear under the bushes and stretched out her cramping legs gratefully as Carter dialed his phone, angled between them so she could hear, too.

"H.O.T. Watch Ops. This is Boo and subject. We have been attacked. Driver's dead. Vehicle down. We're on foot and possibly under pursuit by a hostile hunter/killer team. Request immediate backup."

She expected some sort of exclamation of surprise at that transmission, but all she heard faintly through Carter's phone was a calm, "Say status."

"We're banged up but ambulatory. Fully functional."

He could speak for himself. She felt anything but fully functional at the moment. She felt like she'd just run a marathon and, if she remembered her ancient first-aid training correctly, she was a little bit in shock.

"Roger, Boo. Stand by."

"That's all they've got for us?" she demanded in disgust. "Stand by?"

He smiled grimly. "Oh, trust me. All hell's just broken loose in the bat cave. If I were duty controller today, I'd be on the horn with the FBI and maybe the Marines at Quantico seeing who can scramble a helicopter full of armed SWAT guys the fastest. They'll be swarming this area in a half hour. In the meantime, I might call the state police and local sheriff and see if they can get some units out here sooner."

"Uh, Carter," she murmured. "We may not have that long."

He glanced up and swore quietly. Okay, so she wasn't mistaken. Those *were* a half-dozen men carrying really big guns climbing out of a van right where their SUV had gone into the ditch.

"We'll never outrun them," he whispered. "We're going to have to hide. Fast. Help me."

He carefully lifted a layer of dead, wet leaves aside, doing his best to keep the mats of leaves intact. She mimicked him as best she could. Then he started scrabbling at the earth below with his bare hands. She pitched in, breaking nails and grinding dirt under their remains. Thankfully, the soil was rich and black and soft and gave way easily.

"That's wide enough. Now start lengthening the trench," he whispered. She helped eagerly until he said, "Lie down in it."

"Why?" she asked warily.

"I'm going to bury you."

Oh, God. Her worst nightmare come true. "My claustrophobia!" she gasped.

"I'm sorry. You're going to have to grin and bear it. It's either that or we both die."

Terror unlike anything she'd ever experienced ripped through her. But Carter was adamant. He helped her lie down in the shallow grave—ohgod, ohgod, ohgod—and began shoveling dirt over her quickly.

"You're not going to be with me?" she asked, horrified.

"Can't. I've got to lead them away from you. Lay a false trail to buy us time to slip away. If I'm not back in an hour, go to the road, get out of sight of that van and flag down the first car you can. Call H.O.T. Watch. They'll send someone to get you. Proceed to Camp David without me. You've got to tell them what you know."

"I can't leave you—" she wailed under her breath.

He leaned down and cut her off with a fast, hard kiss. "Be brave, *chère*. Everything depends on you doing this."

She shook with horror from head to toe as he buried her under a foot of dirt and carefully covered his work with the matted leaves. He sprinkled a light covering of dirt over her face and the last batch of leaves descended toward her face. An urge to leap up and run away came over her so powerfully that she wasn't sure she could restrain it.

"I love you, Lily."

And then the leaves pressed down over her face, enclosing her in blackness.

What? Whoa. Love? He *loved* her? The concept distracted her just enough from her panic attack that she was able to force herself to lie still for a moment. Another. She counted to ten in her head.

He *loved* her!

Count to sixty. Exhale slowly. Ignore the taste of dirt and the rotten, wormy smell of the leaves. Count to sixty again. Carter loved her. Her! She could lie here for him. Another sixty count. By God, he didn't get to skate clear of hearing her declare her love to him. She was going to lie here as long as it took to get her chance to blow his mind back. She started imagining different ways she could spring the announcement on him for maximum impact.

And then she heard a sound that made her freeze, every scintilla of her panic rushing back full-force. A male voice had just whispered low…in Russian. She heard swishing like someone was shoving aside branches. Kicking at leaves maybe. The whispered voices drew closer. Good grief. They sounded like they were standing practically on top of her. A faint pressure brushed across the tops of her legs. Oh, my God. Someone had just kicked aside the leaves there. Thank God Carter had insisted on actually burying her or else she'd be staring down the barrel of a gun right now.

She drew in the shallowest, most silent breath she could. Released it with painful care. Another breath. A violent need to hyperventilate was building up inside her. She must not breathe fast. Must control her fear. Must live. For Carter.

The voices retreated a bit. Dizzy with fear and oxygen

deprivation, she took a slightly deeper breath. Another. The spots before her eyes disappeared.

She counted to sixty ten more times before she dared take one delicious, deep breath. She listened as hard as she could, but only silence surrounded her. After counting to sixty another half-dozen times, she heard a tiny, tentative noise. A cricket chirped. A simple little cricket, but she could've cried at the beauty of that sharp, tinny sound. The Russians must be gone if the animals were resuming their regular chorus.

Her thoughts turned then to Carter. Where had he disappeared to? Had he hidden somewhere by now or was he out there running for his life? What if he'd had an episode and was out there somewhere, frozen, without her to help him unwind? Knowing him, he would let the Russians spot him on purpose and then use himself as bait to draw them away from her. He was just that kind of guy. He would always protect the lady, even if it cost him his life.

She alternated praying and counting until she'd judged a half hour had passed. The cavalry ought to be here soon to save the day, shouldn't it? Except only silence reigned around her. What was going on? Her claustrophobia gave way to burning curiosity that threatened to get the best of her. Had Carter not fired that last salvo before he left about loving her, she'd so be out of here right now! She would bet he'd said that intentionally, knowing it was the one thing that would ensure her cooperation with his instructions. Jerk.

And then, just like that, the leaves lifted away from her face. She jolted, startled horribly. *Carter.* She hadn't heard him coming. At all. How did he do that?

He put a finger over his lips, but thankfully began pulling

away the leaves and dirt, freeing her from her prison. In a few seconds she was able to sit up. Her clothes were full of damp, cold dirt, but when Carter wrapped her in a fiercely tight hug, she didn't care.

"Where's the cavalry?" she breathed.

"Some yahoo at the FAA panicked when he heard our report of the poison gas attack and decided to be a hero. He called everyone and their uncle and pushed every panic button they have. Homeland Security had to shut down the airspace over this whole part of the country to chase down that crop duster," he explained in disgust. "No helicopters can get here. Local cops have also been tapped to find the guy. We're on our own for a little while longer."

She grimaced. Could this day get any worse?

"The good news is our Russian friends bit on the false trail I laid and are racing through the woods on a wild-goose chase as we speak."

"So we'll just head for the road and flag down a car to get us out of here?" she asked hopefully.

He flashed her a regretful look. "That van the Russians showed up in probably has a driver and a bunch of radios in it. We're not out of the woods yet."

"Now what?" She had complete faith he would know what to do next.

"We're going to crawl along this tree line for a while and use it for cover. Once we're out of sight of that van, then we can head for the road and get help."

A simple plan in theory, but the execution of it sucked rocks. She was hot and sore and scratched to pieces, covered in even more dirt than she had been before, when Carter finally signaled a stop in front of her.

"You see that tree line up ahead? The one running perpendicular to us, out to the road?"

She nodded, too exhausted to speak.

"We'll crawl to that and then follow it out to the road."

She groaned under her breath, her entire body screaming its protest at being forced onward. "I was going to tell you I loved you back. But you can forget that. I hate your guts."

Carter looked back at her sharply. His face froze in shock for a moment, and then he broke into a big grin.

"By the way, how'd you manage to keep going without tensing up when those Russians were chasing you?" she asked him, disgruntled.

"I had a seizure," he admitted low. "I just thawed faster than I used to. I was lucky. I'd gotten enough of a head start on them that by then they were already off following my false trail."

Lucky, indeed. He started crawling again all too soon. She told herself it was for a good cause. Saving the world was more important than her pain. But that didn't make it hurt one bit less. This being a hero stuff was for the birds. Carter could have it.

Several eternities later, Carter stopped and she looked up wearily to spy a ditch yawning before him. They'd made it. The road. Now to convince someone to stop and pick them up.

They must have lain there for ten minutes before she heard the sound of a vehicle coming along. But it wasn't an automobile. It was louder. Punctuated by a steady pop-pop-popping sound. Carter grinned beside her. He must recognize whatever it was.

A big, old, rusty tractor chugged into sight. It was pulling a huge set of plows, folded up at the moment behind the tractor.

Carter jumped up and waved his arms at the farmer

and the man stopped the tractor. She joined Carter when he gestured.

"We could use a ride, mister," Carter yelled. He pulled out his military ID. "I'm in the army and we're in trouble."

"You got something to do with all those cops flying up and down the highway a while back?" the white-haired man challenged.

"We're running from the bad guys all those folks are chasing. On my word of honor, sir, we're the good guys. And we desperately need your help."

"Climb up."

Lily blinked as Carter slid between the giant tire and the diesel engine and nimbly jumped up on what looked like the tire's axle housing. He held a hand down to her, grinning. Hesitantly, she took it and he hoisted her up beside him and shouted over the din of the engine, "I'm Carter, and this is my girl, Lily."

"Pleased to meet you, miss," the farmer shouted.

They putt-putted down the road for maybe a quarter mile. The tractor slowed and the farmer shouted, "Let me just drop off this plow and then I'll take you up to the house and we'll sort out your troubles."

Carter jumped down to help the guy unhitch the plow. Apparently, he had some experience around farm equipment because he seemed to know what he was doing. In a few moments, they took off across the field, away from the road. Carter must have suggested the guy go cross-country to get home. Good idea. Less exposure to possible Russian death squads.

The farmer's house was a modest, one-story affair, a tidy little cottage tucked under a grove of big, old sycamore trees. The man's wife came out on the porch to stare at them as they walked up to the house from the big red barn.

The woman welcomed them inside and poured them tall glasses of made-from-scratch lemonade and insisted on serving them slices of the strawberry pie she'd made for supper. Carter stepped outside to update H.O.T. Watch Ops and request a vehicle out here to pick them up and take them to Camp David.

"Handsome young man," the farmer's wife commented to Lily. "Looks like good people," she added sagely.

Lily smiled. "He is a fine man."

"He seems to like you well enough. Never takes his eyes off you when you're not looking."

Lily smiled, her insides all tingly at the thought of Carter being fascinated by her.

"Sure as I'm sitting here that young feller's smitten with you."

"From your lips to God's ears," Lily murmured.

"Oh, so you like him back, do you?" The woman laughed. "Well, good luck with him. He looks the type to lead the ladies on a merry chase."

Lily laughed, too. "Believe me. He's led me on the merriest of chases. You have no idea."

Carter stepped back inside. "They'll have someone here in a little while. I hate to impose on your hospitality any longer than we have to, but it'll give me an excuse to have another slice of that amazing pie of yours, ma'am."

Lily smiled at how his Southern accent got so much more pronounced when he was flirting like that. The farmer's wife simpered and fluttered and ate up every bit of it, which only encouraged Carter to lay on the charm even thicker. Before they got out of here, the woman was going to have emptied her entire refrigerator onto his plate.

The couple really was lovely, and she enjoyed sitting in their neat little living room listening to their easy banter with Carter. This was the stuff everyday life was made of. People going about their daily routines, making a living, creating a home and growing old together. Sharing a meal with a stranger out of the goodness of their hearts. What she wouldn't give to have this with Carter. But as it was, she didn't even know if any of them would be alive at this time tomorrow.

It took about two hours, but when their ride came, it really came. A half-dozen big, black SUVs similar to the one that had crashed so disastrously earlier, pulled into the open barnyard.

"Who'd you say you were, boy?" the farmer exclaimed. "It looks like the whole FBI came to get you!"

"Actually, they're Secret Service," Carter replied, grinning. "Thanks for everything. And I'll have my mother send you that recipe for rhubarb pie right away."

And as quickly as their unexpectedly pleasant interlude had begun, it ended. She and Carter were stuffed into one of the vehicles, and the whole cavalcade pulled out without further ado. The SUVs drove fast, changing positions every few minutes. Sometimes they were first in line, sometimes last, sometimes in the middle. The men in the car with them made no secret of having their weapons drawn and scanned the road and sky constantly with binoculars. It was nerve-wracking stuff to realize someone might want them dead badly enough to tangle with this bunch.

She glanced over at Carter. He seemed relaxed enough. "No symptoms?" she asked quietly.

"Nope. That last piece of strawberry pie did the trick."

She made a face at him. This was no time for joking around. But he seemed as cool as a cucumber. Finally, she asked under her breath, "Shouldn't you be at least a little nervous?"

"I'm definitely nervous, but it takes a lot more than it used to for me to lock up. And besides, have you seen how these guys are armed?"

Despite his calm, she was tense for the nearly two-hour ride. Finally, the convoy slowed and turned onto a narrow road. In a few minutes, it turned onto an even narrower and, this time, dirt road.

"Looks like we're coming in the back door," Carter commented to her.

"The back door to what?"

"Camp David, of course."

She looked up sharply. All she saw were trees and more trees. And then, without warning, the road turned and a Fort Knox-like fence loomed in front of them. Even in the company of the Secret Service itself, it still took them a while to get through all the security checks at the gate.

"Time?" Carter murmured to her.

She didn't have to ask him what he meant. "Fourteen hours."

He winced. "We could be cutting it close."

"Why? That's plenty of time to convince someone here to call someone there and shut down their machine."

He said quietly, "Systems like that don't just shut down. I'm sure there will be an elaborate protocol they'll have to go through to convince the machine that it's receiving a legitimate order to shut itself off. It'll have layer after layer of encryption and fail-safes designed to keep everyone but a very few authorized people from pulling the plug."

She gasped in dismay. "How long could that take?"

He shrugged. "Anywhere from a few minutes to hours. Worst case, we've got to assume it'll take the Russians several hours. For that matter, the Russian prime minister won't be able to just pick up the phone and give an order like that. He'll no doubt have to go through some sort of procedure to verify his orders with his subordinates."

"Good grief," she exclaimed. Were they already too late?

Chapter 12

Time seemed to alternately fly at double or triple speed, and then slow down to a maddening crawl as she waited impatiently for Carter to talk his way through the various layers of security surrounding the president and his cabinet. Apparently, someone named General Wittenauer had made some phone calls and greased the skids, but there were still protocols to be followed before anyone spoke to the president.

Lily still couldn't quite believe she was going to brief the president. In person. And she'd thought giving the oral defense of her dissertation had been nerve-wracking!

Someone, a younger man in a dark suit, explained it to her and Carter. "You'll brief the chief of staff first. He'll prep you with any questions he has and you'll want to incorporate whatever information he asks for into your final briefing. Assuming he sees no serious problems with the material, you'll then brief the president. Be concise. Get to the point. Don't waste his time."

Lily nodded numbly and clung to Carter's hand tightly. She could do this. She'd endured being buried alive. How bad could it be to talk to a man who was reported to be imminently reasonable and intelligent? The president was just another American citizen. Right? Just a really, really powerful and important one.

Carter briefed the chief of staff about the intelligence that led H.O.T. Watch to believe a doomsday device, indeed, existed. Most of that information she'd never heard before. It was convincing to say the least. Then she was up to bat. She stumbled and stammered, but the chief of staff seemed so appalled by their presentation that he barely asked any questions. He merely nodded when the aide asked if they were cleared to present their briefing.

The aide replied, "The president is just finishing up supper. Can you wait a half hour?"

Lily surprised herself by answering firmly, "No, we can't. We've jumped through all of your hoops and been as cooperative as we can be. But no. We need to speak to the president right now. Time is of the absolute essence."

"She's right," the chief of staff declared. "Tell the boss to skip dessert. This briefing's going to give him a serious case of indigestion anyway."

The aide looked alarmed and left the room hastily.

Lily glanced over at Carter. He smiled at her, but the expression didn't reach his eyes. It was time to do or die. She murmured, "Hey, at least this place probably has a great bomb shelter. If they'll let us in, we'll live long enough to see the nuclear winter."

"Yippee," Carter muttered. "I think I'd rather go in the first wave. Quick and painless, and then it's over. I'm not into long, drawn-out suffering."

She supposed he would know. He'd been through plenty of it in the past few months.

"Okay, you're on," the aide told them as he returned. "The first lady is just leaving the dining room and then I'll walk you in."

"I'll walk them in," the chief of staff said grimly.

A few seconds later, a silent Secret Service man opened the door and gestured them through it. And in about a dozen steps, she was standing in front of the president of the United States at the dinner table. She vaguely registered the faces of a dozen other people at the table—the assembled cabinet members.

The chief of staff said soberly, "Sir, these young people have quite a story to tell you."

The president stood up, offered his hand to Carter and then to her. "I'm Henry Stanforth. I'm interested to hear what's got the staff in such a tizzy. Please, sit down."

Someone stepped forward to whisk the remaining dinner dishes out of the way as Lily murmured, "I think I'd rather stand, sir. I'm too nervous to sit still."

He smiled kindly at her. "I won't bite your head off. Just tell me what you came to say."

Carter started into his briefing. He, too, was stiff at first, but then warmed to his topic and smoothly went through the documentation and evidence H.O.T. Watch had gathered to prove the doomsday machine existed. He then gave a quick overview of what H.O.T. Watch believed it would do if activated and what the conditions were under which it would fire.

And then it was her turn. Familiar to her from television, a keenly intelligent pair of hazel eyes speared into her. She took a deep breath and then spoke. "Well, sir. It all started with an asteroid. An insignificant little chunk of rock, really…"

It took her a few minutes, but somewhere along the way, as the president asked an occasional question and nodded in comprehension at her explanations, she began to relax. At least as much as it was possible to relax when standing in front of the president of the United States and telling him the world was going to end in a few hours.

She finished, and the room was dead silent.

"Well, then," Stanforth finally said quietly. "It seems like we've got a problem on our hands. What do you want me to do about it?"

Carter answered, "I…we…need you to contact the Russian prime minister. You've got to convince him to turn the machine off ASAP."

Stanforth leaned back in his chair, thinking. Lily felt the man's mind at work, turning over all the possibilities. No doubt he was already formulating the best arguments to use to convince the Russian prime minister and weighing which ones would succeed or fail.

"Comments?" Stanforth asked.

Lily started. She'd been so mesmerized by him that she'd nearly forgotten the entire cabinet was also in the room. A man she recognized as the secretary of defense, but whose name she couldn't remember for the life of her at the moment, replied. "Time is of the essence. I don't think we should let this thing get too bogged down in discussion and options before you act. Seems to me these young people have done their homework and exhausted every other reasonable avenue for contacting the Russians."

"Boris is going to have a cow when I reveal to him that we know about their little device," Stanforth commented mildly. "It's quite an intelligence edge for us to just give away."

The national security adviser grimaced. "I'd say in the current circumstances the sacrifice is worth it, sir."

"Never thought I'd hear you say something so sensible,

Tom," Stanforth replied. There were chuckles up and down the table.

"Well, then. It seems this is a call for the red phone," Stanforth announced quietly.

There was an audible intake of breath in the room. Lily recalled dimly that the red phone was supposed to be used only in case of impending nuclear war or times of extreme crisis on that scale. Wow.

A man in a navy uniform stepped forward immediately and laid a briefcase on the table in front of the president. Lily was startled to see that it really was handcuffed to the guy's wrist. The navy officer dialed in a pair of combinations and the lid popped open. And, indeed, a red telephone lay there. She imagined the technology behind it had been updated substantially since the thing had been invented, but it was still an old-fashioned red handset.

President Stanforth picked it up and murmured a string of letters and numbers into it. "How do you put this thing on speakerphone?" he asked.

The navy man leaned forward and pushed a button. A female voice with a faint Russian accent said, "Stand by for the prime minister, Mr. President."

A male voice said something in Russian that sounded like letters and numbers. And then the voice said, "Henry, why do you wake me up at this hour to speak on the red phone?"

Lily didn't know the prime minster spoke English so well. It must make communications between these two powerful men easier without having to rely on translators.

"Boris, I'm sorry to wake you up."

Lily listened for the next several minutes as President Stanforth did a masterful job of explaining the crisis without ever putting the prime minister in a situation to have to confirm or deny the existence of the doomsday machine.

Finally, the Russian said heavily, "It is extraordinary story you tell me, Henry. You understand I must speak to my army about this."

"Just do it quickly, Boris. You may have only an hour or two to get the shut-down sequence started in time to avoid disaster. Assuming such a sequence of events turns out to be necessary, of course."

"Of course. I will be in touch. *Dobrii vecher,* Henry."

"Good night, Boris. I'll wait for your call."

Carter thought time had moved slowly during those terrible two weeks when he'd been completely paralyzed and unsure if he would ever be able to move again. But this, this was worse.

He and Lily had been escorted to a homey room stuffed with books of all kinds, and they sat side-by-side on a couch, staring at a selection of popular paperback novels. He couldn't remember any of their titles two seconds after reading them. By mutual unspoken consent, they'd agreed to ignore the elephant in the corner for now—their earlier declarations of love would have to wait until later. After they'd saved the world.

"How're you holding up?" Lily startled him by leaning close to murmur.

"Okay under the circumstances, I suppose."

"No sign of a seize-up?"

He shook his head, and she, in turn, looked surprised. Now that he thought about it, he guessed he was, too. Standing in front of the president and his cabinet by all rights should have sent him into full-blown statue mode. But he'd gotten through it. He'd told himself that Lily was depending on him and he couldn't let her down. Surely his cure wasn't as simple as that. Some woman loved him, so now it was all better?

Except that woman was Lily, and she was anything but "some woman." She was extraordinary in just about every way.

The debate raged in his head until a Secret Service man cleared his throat in the doorway. "You're needed in the conference room."

Carter helped Lily to her feet and the two of them followed their guide to a state-of-the-art teleconferencing room. The cabinet members were trickling in and standing in small clusters, talking quietly.

"What's happening?" Lily whispered to him.

"The Russian prime minister must be about to call back."

He heard Lily's gulp and knew the feeling. He had to believe the Russians were sensible people with no desire to allow a global catastrophe. They would turn off the machine.

A door on the far side of the room opened, and everyone turned. The president walked in and took his seat at the head of the table. "I'm told my Russian counterpart expects to make a call to me momentarily."

The cabinet members took their places and an aide gestured Carter and Lily to chairs along one side of the room. Her hand crept into his and he gripped it reassuringly.

"Greetings, Henry." The Russian prime minister's voice came through the surround-sound speakers in the room.

"Hello, Boris. You have good news for me, I hope?" President Stanforth replied.

"This is very interesting report you send me. My scientists take some time to verify the mathematics. They send compliments to Dr. James on her work. My staff also finds your Captain Baigneaux's conclusions plausible, if rather far-fetched."

Stanforth made an impatient sound. "Then you are absolutely satisfied that no threat exists? I can go to bed tonight with your full assurance that I will wake up tomorrow to just another normal day?"

The Russian prime minister didn't hesitate. "You have my absolute assurance of it, my friend. There will be no accidental launch of anything as a result of this asteroid of yours. I have seen to it personally."

Stanforth made a slashing gesture with a hand across his throat, and a man seated at a computer console in the corner nodded. "You are off speakerphone, Mr. President."

"Do we all take that to be the Russians saying they've turned the thing off?"

Nods passed all around the table.

"Captain Baigneaux?" Stanforth was looking right at him. "Are you satisfied?"

Tension climbed the back of his legs ominously. But then Lily's hand squeezed his, and the seizure retreated, the monster sliding back into the abyss for the moment. "It's not my call to make, sir. But, yes. That is how I would interpret his remarks. Shy of forcing him to admit outright if the device exists, this is the best assurance we can expect from him."

Stanforth nodded. "I'm not willing to force him to make that concession as long as the damn thing's turned off."

The president gestured to the technician again. "Boris, I am relieved to hear this. I have always said you are a reasonable and intelligent man."

A gust of laughter filled the room. "Henry, you and I both know you think I am a born-again bastard whom you would spit on rather than save from drowning."

Stanforth grinned. "Now, now, Boris. I'd save you from drowning…after I spit on you."

The Russian laughed. "Thank you for bringing this situation to my attention, Henry."

"My pleasure. Thank you for looking into it so promptly."

"Speaking of which, I have question for you. Where do you hear of this supposed device of ours?"

"The pictures of the asteroid came from the Hubble, I believe," Stanforth answered, looking over to Carter for confirmation. Carter nodded, wincing. He saw where this was going, and there was no way to get out of this conversation well. He made a cutoff gesture at the president.

"One moment, Boris. My aides are confirming the source of the photographs."

The technician went off speakerphone.

"What's up, Captain?" Stanforth asked sharply.

"Some of the pictures and all of the information about the doomsday machine came from a highly classified surveillance facility that our government does not acknowledge exists."

"And?"

"Sir, I believe the Russian prime minister is about to ask you about it point-blank. Maybe he wants to even the playing field now that we know about the doomsday machine. He wants us to verify the existence of H.O.T. Watch to him."

"And you want me to lie to him about it?"

Carter winced. "In a word, yes."

Stanforth leaned back in his chair. "The balance of world power is extremely delicate, son. As you saw tonight, trust between world leaders is imperative in situations exactly like this one. Boris and I have to know we will always speak truthfully with one another. We may speak in diplomatic hyperbole, and we may evade various issues with great care, but we do not lie."

"Then, sir, I respectfully offer myself as the sacrificial lamb."

"I beg your pardon?" Stanforth looked startled.

Carter had no idea what came over him. Maybe it was that foolishly heroic streak that drew him and most of his kind to the Special Forces in the first place. "You're going to need a fall guy. Fast. And I'm offering to be it. Tell the Russians I infiltrated Siberia and got the data on the doomsday machine. They'll come after me as a matter of retribution, but H.O.T. Watch will be safe, everyone's honor will be served, and your delicate balance of power will be maintained."

Stanforth stared at him hard. "Are you sure?"

"Yes, sir."

Lily was all but crushing his hand, but to her credit, she said nothing. She understood why he had to do this. He might be done as a field operative. He might be screwed up in the head and carrying a burden of guilt he wouldn't shed in a lifetime of trying. He might be a mere husk of the man he'd once been. But he could do this. He could die for his country.

And what more could he ask for? What more could any man ask for than for his death to have great meaning? If he protected the secret of H.O.T. Watch with his life, countless other lives would be saved by the facility's continued ability to function in secret.

Stanforth gestured at the technician and spoke to the Russian prime minister again. "I'm told by my staff that although the pictures came from Hubble, the other information in the report came from direct observation.

Captain Baigneaux is with me right now and he vouches for all the data personally."

Lily leaned close to breathe, "What does that mean?"

"Stanforth just told the Russians I personally collected the intel on the doomsday machine by infiltrating the facility it's housed in."

"But you didn't—" She fell silent, her expression horrified. Then she breathed, "They'll kill you."

"They can try. They've already failed to get you several times and me twice. I'm feeling confident about my odds."

"But—"

He gestured her to silence. The Russian prime minister was speaking angrily. "...take a very dim view of such operations against our nation...must express our outrage and protest in the strongest possible terms..."

Carter tuned out. Fair warning being served by the Russians that they planned to eliminate him. A few old-school spies were left who played the game in a marginally gentlemanly way. Apparently, the Russian prime minister was one of them. Carter's jaw tightened. Message received, loud and clear. He was about to go to ground for a very long time. Alone.

But there was one more thing he had to do first. He had to say goodbye to Lily. And of everything he'd had to face on this mission, he dreaded that the worst of all.

Chapter 13

Carter closed the door to their casually chic Camp David bedroom behind Lily, wincing as he waited for the explosion to come.

"Are you nuts, Carter?" she demanded angrily.

"It's my job. My duty. You don't have to like what I did, but it's done now. And," he added, "I'd do it again if I had the choice."

She glared at him for good measure, but she knew when she was beat in an argument of logic. "I still don't like it," she announced.

"I don't like it either, but it was necessary to protect H.O.T. Watch."

She sighed.

"The good news is we got the machine turned off," he said in a blatant attempt to distract her. It worked.

"We did it, didn't we?" A smile broke across her face.

He smiled back at her. "Seems like it."

"Is the world really safe? We'll go to bed tonight and wake up tomorrow just like nothing happened?"

"Well, I hear a few rabbits in Siberia aren't going to have a very good day tomorrow."

"Sad, isn't it? They didn't asked to be squished."

"Better them than us."

"Still…"

He thought it was sweet that she was worried about the bunnies, but really. "Lily, take a perspective check. Rabbits breed and die by the thousands every day on Earth. You just saved the lives of seven billion human beings. A few rabbits are not worth getting all worked up about."

She nodded, serious for a moment, and then she twirled in a circle and laughed at the ceiling. "We really did it! The rest of our lives are waiting for us. Family and friends and kids and… Oh, and I can get tenure, and then I can tell Bill Kaplan to take a long hike off a short pier. And I can find out if my calculations about the impact were accurate. And I'm going to Venice. I'm not putting it off any longer. As soon as the school year ends, I'm traveling. Come with me."

He'd had a chat with Jennifer Blackfoot before they'd come back to their room about that very subject. Lily fancied herself in love with him now, but he had faith she'd get over her infatuation once they'd been apart for a few months. He knew her well enough to be dead sure she wouldn't let him go into hiding alone without a fight. So he'd decided to be proactive about it.

"Speaking of travel," he said casually, "how would you feel about going to Siberia to have a look at the damage your asteroid caused?"

She stopped dancing around to stare at him. "I beg your pardon?"

"I had a little talk with the folks at H.O.T. Watch while

the president was thanking you for saving the day. Turns out the U.S. government would like to fund your ongoing research into asteroid and meteor damage forecasting. They're as interested as you are in seeing just how accurate your algorithms turn out to be. How would you like to tell Bill Kaplan to take his tenure and shove it, and instead go to H.O.T. Watch headquarters and continue your work from there?"

"That would be amazing! You'll come with me, right?"

He shook his head. "I'm going to be persona non grata with the Russians for a while. They're going to be looking for me, and I can't lead them to the H.O.T. Watch facility."

"Too bad we can't watch the asteroid hit from H.O.T. Watch headquarters."

"I actually might be able to arrange that. They have the capability to send images just about anywhere, and I hear there's pretty good technical capability around this place."

She grinned at him. "Really?"

"Let me make another call." He got Jennifer on the phone again and she readily agreed to his request to point one of H.O.T. Watch's cameras at Siberia the following afternoon.

Lily was waiting impatiently when he hung up the phone, all but bouncing on the edge of the bed.

He grinned and leaned down over her, forcing her to lie back. As he followed her down to the mattress, he paused, his mouth inches from hers. "What's it worth to you to see that asteroid hit?"

"A back rub for you."

He considered, frowning. "That's all?"

"A back rub and I'll finally model that red teddy."

"That's better, but still not quite good enough."

She gave him one of her flirty looks out of the corner of her eye that never failed to make his gut tighten. "Okay, then. This is my final offer. A back rub, the red teddy and you get to do whatever you want with me for the next hour."

The idea made his whole body clench in anticipation. He laughed. "Now you're talking."

"You're sure it's not inappropriate to fool around in a place like this?" she whispered.

"What? You mean in a bedroom?"

She slapped his upper arm lightly. "No! Camp David."

"I expect President Stanforth is celebrating the same way we are right about now."

"Eww. I didn't need that visual image."

"Just because he's president doesn't mean the guy's a monk."

"Still, it's like thinking about your parents having sex." She shuddered dramatically.

He kissed all that joy flowing from her, absorbing it straight into his soul. He was going to miss this about her.

But then her arms came around him and she kissed him back, and maybe that was what he was going to miss about her most. Her tongue stroked his lips, inviting him to come and play in her garden of delights, tempting him to taste her. She grew more bold and he opened for her. Her fingers laced into his hair, tugging him closer so that she could plunge her tongue into his mouth and engage in a duel that left him breathless.

"I surrender," he mumbled against her honey-tasting mouth.

"Surrender? You're *surrendering,* Mr. Big Bad Soldier?"

"You do have some mouth on you for an astrophysicist."

"And what *are* you planning to do with it?" she asked saucily.

He wrapped his arms around her and rolled with her until she was sprawled beneath him in the middle of the bed. That red teddy might just have to wait a while tonight. One thing he knew for sure, that boring suit had to go. But not until he had her hair down out of that uptight bun.

Hairpins went flying as she laughed in protest. "Don't you like the schoolmarm look? I thought all boys have naughty fantasies about their teachers."

"Maybe if you're their teacher, they do. You should have seen the guys in your class that first day I saw you. They were all but drooling on their notebooks. I bet half the males in your class don't give a flying flip about astronomy. They were there to look at you, Professor."

A blush climbed her cheeks, and he kissed it across her face and down her throat to its source. "I'd have been an astronomer for sure, if you'd been at MIT," he murmured.

"Yeah, but I always went for the math geeks."

He grinned against the hollow of her throat. "So all I have to do is whisper quadratic equations in your ear and you'll melt in my hands?"

"Oh baby, oh baby, oh. If you whisper a Fourier series to me, I'll go positively wild. Calculate parallax on a distant star and I'm yours forever."

God, he was going to miss the laughter.

"Stick with me, sugar, and I'll show you the stars."

"Hey, that's my line!"

She'd already shown him the stars and beyond. He figured he owed her one last trip around the universe before he destroyed hers. He took her clothes off slowly, peeling away the wool and silk by inches, kissing each bit of flesh as it was tantalizingly revealed. Lily was squirming with impatience by the time he finally disrobed her. She didn't understand. He was memorizing every inch of her, every sigh, every whiff of peaches and cream and honey, every satin-smooth contour of her flesh.

He was a damn fool for putting himself in a position to have to leave this. But what choice did he have? Duty resonated from the very depths of his soul. Honor. Country. It wasn't what he did; it was who he was.

It was time for him to face facts. He was never going to be a field operator again. His head wasn't in the game any longer and he would never be able to be certain if and when he would have a freeze-up. Life as he knew it was over. He'd had a good run. Saved the world. He supposed he was okay with checking out of the mortal coil. But he damn well wouldn't ask that of Lily. She had so much life in her. So much living to do. Who knew what contributions she would make to the field of science in the remainder of her career?

No way was he going to endanger Lily's life by inviting her to go with him when he ran. He shouldn't have tried to tough out protecting her as it was. They were incredibly lucky to still be alive. But no more. If he really cared about her, he would let her go for her own safety. Let her get over him and get on with her life. He loved her. He'd rather live without her than see her harmed.

And besides, what kind of life would it be for her? Living under an assumed name. Having to abandon her family, her work and her research. Never sure from day to day if someone was about to show up and kill them. It was no way to live. How could they even think about having children and subjecting them to that sort of danger? They'd never have any kind of a normal life. He couldn't do that to her.

She deserved better than him. She deserved someone who could be there for her all the time. Someone who wouldn't threaten to turn into a statue every time the going got rough. Hell, who wouldn't bring killers to her doorstep. It was a bitter pill to swallow.

"Earth to Carter. Come in, please."

"What?" He blinked down at her.

"You checked out on me for a second there. Everything okay?"

He sighed. "Yes, I'm fine. The past few days have just made me think about a lot of things."

"I know the feeling. Thinking you're about to die sort of reduces life down to the essentials, doesn't it?"

He smiled down at her, his heart in his throat. "Yeah, it does."

"Is that why you do a job like this? To feel this alive?"

"It's certainly one of the side benefits."

"Well, then, let's get on with celebrating being alive, already. You, sir, are far too clothed for my taste."

"Oh, really? And what do you plan to do about it, short stuff?"

She shoved at his shoulders and he rolled over obligingly. She treated him to the same slow, kiss-laden stripping that he'd subjected her to, and he all but quivered with need before she was done with him. But he supposed he deserved it. Turn about was fair play.

She crawled across his chest, her firm, pert breasts pushing against him. "Carter?"

"Hmm?"

"Make love to me like the world's still about to end."

"Honey, the world is about to end. We're leaving this planet behind and heading out into your precious cosmos and never coming back." God, if only they could. He'd go with her in a second.

Then her hands were on him, her tight, soft fist sending him out of his mind like it always did. She murmured to him all of the things she wanted to do with him, all the things she wanted to try, all the things she'd never dared tell anyone about before. And as she poured out her most private and personal secrets for him, he died a little inside. What he wouldn't give to be there for her, to make all her most treasured dreams come true. He already hated with a passion the man who got to do that for her.

But he had tonight. And he damn well planned to make as many of her dreams come true as he could before it was time for him to leave and break her heart. At least he hoped his leaving would break her heart a little.

He pulled her up against him, fitting their bodies together and then rolling over to plunge into all her glorious heat and uninhibited passion. He reached between them to tease her to a fever pitch and she danced upon his fingers, keening out her pleasure and need. He drank in all her cries, kissing her as if she was the air he breathed.

They took off like a rocket into the night, all roaring fire and blasting smoke and sparks, and he rode the rumbling explosion of their love up and out of the atmosphere into forever. Nothing existed but the two of them, fused into one heart, one soul. One explorer seeking and finding the farthest reaches of the universe. Love expanded in his heart to fill the entire void until he was bursting with it. Like the big bang, it exploded free of him, bursting over the two of them with all the apocalyptic glory of creation.

Carter collapsed, stunned, vaguely registering something wet on his face. He reached up and wiped away the tear tracks running down his cheeks. He'd cried over the deaths of those children. Had cried for their lost innocence, their lost childhoods. And he'd cried for the women they'd murdered. Women who'd loved and lost little boys to man's brutality.

But this grief went so deep into his soul that he couldn't give words to it. Having Lily was perfection almost too much for his soul to comprehend—and losing her was unlike any agony he'd ever suffered. It went so far beyond pain he almost couldn't grasp it.

"Whew," she murmured, wiping perspiration off her forehead. "Is this room hot, or am I having a hot flash?"

"It's possible we actually expended a fair bit of physical energy," he replied roughly, praying she'd mistake any remaining wetness on his face as merely perspiration left over from their passionate sex.

"Mmm. My kind of aerobics," she murmured, sounding sleepy.

He gathered her close to his side, cradling her in his arms one last time. She snuggled against him sleepily and drifted off, her breathing light and even. He held her for a long time—until he had no more hot, silent tears left in him. And then, as dawn crept around the edges of the curtains, he eased out from under her, pressed one last gentle kiss upon her forehead, got dressed quietly and slipped out of her life.

Chapter 14

Lily woke up nested deep within a down comforter in a comfortable bed. Where was she? Her mind swam slowly toward consciousness. What time was it? She rolled over and squinted at the alarm clock on the nightstand until the numbers came into focus. Ten twenty-two. The faintest trace of light crept around the window shades. It was morning, then.

Where was Carter?

The blankets on his side of the bed were pulled up neatly, but the down pillow still held an impression of his head. She reached out to touch the spot and was surprised to feel dampness there. He'd made love to her so tenderly, so sweetly last night that he'd nearly brought her to tears. They'd both been so relieved that the crisis had been solved she figured her emotion was partly because of that.

Except something had been different in the way he held her. In the way he never took his eyes off her. As if he was trying to memorize everything about her. The way she looked, the way she felt and smelled and tasted.

She sat up in bed and gazed around in the gloom. His clothes were gone. He must have decided to let her sleep and gotten up to get a bite to eat. But a vibration of alarm started low in her gut.

She got up and dressed quickly. She was getting really tired of Washington lawyer power suits—one of the female staffers had lent her this one to brief the president in last night. A Secret Service man at the end of the hallway greeted her when she emerged from the bedroom. Maybe she'd get to tell her grandkids someday about sleeping in Camp David, too.

"Excuse me," she asked the agent, "do you know where I can find Captain Baigneaux?"

"I believe he left the compound several hours ago, ma'am."

The vibration became a louder hum of alarm in her gut. "I need to get in touch with him. Can you tell me how I might do that?"

"Let me take you to the comm center, ma'am."

She followed the big man down a hallway to a smallish room crammed with computers and telephones and gear whose purpose she didn't have the faintest idea of.

"I need to get in touch with Captain Baigneaux," she said tightly.

Those were definitely sympathetic looks the technicians were sending her way. Did everyone know something she didn't? Okay, now she was starting to freak out. One of the techs held out a headset for her. She donned it nervously.

"H.O.T. Watch headquarters is coming on the line now, ma'am."

Why H.O.T. Watch? She'd asked for Carter. A male voice

spoke in her ear. Not the one she wanted to hear, though. "Lily?"

"Brady?" Her heart climbed into her throat while her soul plummeted to the floor. "Where's Carter?"

"He had to go to ground for a while. Till he cools off a bit."

"What the hell does that mean?" she snapped. "I'm a civilian, remember? I don't speak your lingo."

"Right. Sorry. Some folks may try to harm him and he's lying low—staying out of sight. Hiding, if you will—for a while."

"How are you planning to get me to him, then?" she asked matter-of-factly.

"Excuse me?"

"You heard me. If you think I'm letting him go through that alone, you're sadly mistaken, Commander."

"Lily, you can't be with him."

She spoke patiently. "Have I not done absolutely everything you asked of me ever since Carter picked me up at my campus?"

"Yes," Brady answered cautiously.

Her voice rose a little. "Have I not put my *life* on the line more than once to help you people solve your crisis?"

"Yes." Outright nervousness resonated in his voice now.

"Did I or did I not directly help to *save the world* last night?"

"That is correct." Brady was starting to sound desperate.

She said forcefully, "Then do you or do you not owe me a *gigantic* favor?"

"Of course, but—"

She cut him off. "No buts. You know what I want. I expect you to make it happen."

"I would if I could, but it's impossible—"

"Brady Hathaway," she declared reproachfully, "H.O.T. Watch's specialty is the impossible. Am I right?"

"You're killing me here, Lily."

"Then shut up and deliver, buster. I'll be waiting for your call when you've made the arrangements."

As she disconnected the call, she caught the grins the Camp David comm techs were hiding as they turned away from her quickly.

She shook her head and muttered, "You just have to know how to handle these military men. A woman has to be firm with them or they think they can get away with murder. I'm expecting a call back from Commander Hathaway in a little while. You'll let me know when it comes in?"

"Yes, ma'am," one of the techs managed to get out past his choked laughter.

Lily marched out of the comm center, and the Secret Service agent outside the door was grinning. "Are you hungry, ma'am?" he asked.

"Yes, I am."

If Carter Baigneaux thought he was just going to up and run away to be all heroic and tortured by himself, he could think again. He was her man and there was no way on God's green Earth she was letting him get away from her that easily.

She ate brunch, and it was probably very tasty, but she didn't notice. A staff member took her plate away, but no call had come yet. She occupied herself having a little chat with one of the female aides, who was more than happy to provide whatever Lily needed for the next leg of her journey.

She was surprised, though, when the beautiful suitcase and its contents arrived in her room an hour later. They were presented to her along with a handwritten thank-you note from Henry Stanforth personally. The president's note did not refer to any specifics of the crisis, but merely thanked her in the warmest possible terms on behalf of a grateful nation for her service to her country. She guessed that would shut up the grandkids in fifty years or so. She tucked the note away carefully among her new clothes, including several very short miniskirts.

A knock sounded on her door. "Ma'am, you've got a call. Commander Hathaway—"

Lily was already out the door.

"Hi, Lily. It's Brady."

"What's the plan?"

"I'm going to meet you in Washington, D.C., to-night—"

"And then you'll take me to him?"

"And then we'll talk," he said firmly.

She scowled. Apparently, Carter's boss could be as stubborn as he. But she was no amateur at handling difficult men who wouldn't give her what she wanted.

"Brady, I have an idea."

"Uh-oh."

"What would happen if we let the Russians kill Carter?"

"Excuse me?" Brady exclaimed incredulously.

"Well, more precisely, what if we let them *think* they'd succeeded in killing Carter? Would they back off and go home?"

"Of course. If they thought their mission was accomplished, they'd leave."

"So, then, let's let them think that."

"Easier said than done. They'll want to confirm their kill."

"Then we'll have to stage an explosion or something to make them think Carter's body was destroyed."

"This isn't a television show, Lily. These guys are thorough."

"And so are you. You can do the impossible, remember?"

Brady sighed.

She continued, "If you were the Russians right now, and you were trying to find Carter, how would you do it?"

He paused for several moments, thinking. "I'd stake out Camp David and either wait to follow him, or barring spotting Carter, I'd follow you."

"Exactly! So use me as bait. Take me to Carter and I'll bring the Russians with me. You set up your fake trap with Carter, and I'll join him when it's ready. We let the Russians ambush him, we let them think they've shot him or whatever. Then we blow up the site, Carter and I slip away, and the Russians go home all happy."

"It's not a bad plan in theory, but it's dangerous, Lily. The Russians might just succeed in killing not only him but you, too."

"Do you seriously think I want to live out my life without Carter?" she demanded.

The line went silent. At length, Brady finally said, "Are you sure?"

A female voice cut onto the line, startling Lily. "Of course she's sure, Brady. The woman's in love."

"Thanks, Jennifer," Lily said drily.

"No problem. I say we green-light the plan," Jennifer declared.

"I'm feeling ganged up on here," Brady grumbled. "I won't be bullied into a bad decision. I won't risk one of my best men because you two are all caught up in the romance of the thing."

Jennifer's voice was cold when she replied, "Are you questioning my judgment, Commander?"

He sighed audibly. "I'm just suggesting that we think this through with our heads, not our hearts."

Lily said carefully, "I'm a scientist. I deal in facts. And the fact is, I will do whatever it takes, face whatever risk is necessary, to be with Carter."

"All right, then," he replied heavily. "I'll set it up."

"Oh, and Brady?" Lily added.

"Now what?"

"Don't tell Carter. You know he'll flatly refuse to go along with this."

"Smart man," Brady grumbled.

"Don't make me come down there and kick you in the shins," Lily threatened. "I am going to be with him one way or another."

Brady laughed. "All right, already. Far be it from me to stand in the way of true love. I've already learned not to mess with that with some of my other guys. I give up. We'll do it your way."

"Thank you, Commander," Lily said with heartfelt gratitude.

"Don't thank me. It's your neck on the line."

The asteroid-watching party in the Camp David teleconference room—images supplied courtesy of H.O.T. Watch's finest—was anticlimactic. One second Lily was staring at an expanse of white snow, the next there was a puff of smoke, and when it cleared, a big hole in the ground.

The good news was no alarms went off in the conference room. No DefCon 1 alerts, no racing the president down into some nuclear-proof bunker. All in all, it was a quiet afternoon at the lodge retreat.

And Lily was a mess. With every minute that passed, Carter got farther away from her, both physically and emotionally. She knew him. He'd be talking himself into how he'd done the right thing to leave her behind. How it was the best thing for her. How his sacrifice was all noble and virtuous. She was going to have to smack him around when she caught up with him. Explain to him that true love meant never having to be apart. That she would stick by him through thick and thin, good and bad, safe times and dangerous times. End of discussion. Really, it was that simple.

It was the next morning before Lily left Camp David in a ridiculously conspicuous motorcade complete with police escort cars flashing their lights all the way back to Andrews Air Force Base in the Washington suburbs. If the Russians didn't know where she was after that circus, then they were so incompetent that Carter had nothing to worry about anyway.

She boarded a military business jet in broad daylight, being sure to stand around the ramp for a while first so any observing Russians would have no trouble spotting her. The plane flew her to New Orleans Naval Air Station in time for her to land before sunset.

When she deplaned, muggy heat stole her breath away and curled tendrils of her hair around her face in moments. Carter had grown up in this oppressive climate? No wonder the guy was so laid-back most of the time. Who could do anything fast in this steam bath? It sapped the starch right out of her.

What was Carter doing right now? Did he have any inkling that she was coming after him? Or did he seriously think she would just pack up and go back to her regularly scheduled life without him? A tiny piece of her heart worried that he wouldn't be happy to see her. Or more precisely, that he didn't want to see her again. She had faith he wouldn't be happy when she joined him. Particularly when he found out about the part where she'd led Russian hit men straight to him.

A tall man strode across the tarmac as she headed for the passenger terminal. "Welcome to N'Awlins, Lily."

"Thanks for doing all this for me, Brady. I know I'm being a pain in the butt."

He smiled ruefully. "I can't disagree with you on that score. But Carter's earned it. You both have."

"So, do we know if the Russians have picked me up?"

"Oh, yeah. There was a hack-in of the FAA computers as soon as your airplane took off from Andrews. They know where your plane was headed."

She looked around reflexively.

"They probably don't have a man on this base directly. But they'll be waiting for us as soon as we leave the Naval Air Station," Brady commented.

"When are we going?"

"As soon as it gets dark. We'll be easier to follow then."

She laughed at the strange expression that crossed his face. "Not used to saying that, are you?"

"This is a rather strange operation. I don't usually go out of my way to be followed, no. But then, I don't usually blow up one of my men either."

"It's all for a good cause."

He smiled back wryly. "I wouldn't know. I've managed to avoid romantic entanglements over the course of my career."

"There's a first time for everything, Commander." She added slyly, "And you do realize you've just jinxed yourself, right?"

He scowled. "Nope, not me. I'm not a relationship kind of guy."

Laughing, she retorted, "Yup, you're definitely jinxed now."

"C'mon." He grabbed her suitcase and headed for an open-roofed Jeep at the edge of the parking ramp.

"You're taking me?" she asked, surprised. "Aren't you the supervisor?"

"I didn't get that position by sitting on my…behind. I'm as qualified to operate in the field as my men. And this one is too important to risk anybody else screwing it up. The timing's going to be delicate if we're to avoid blowing the two of you to smithereens."

She winced at the notion, and Brady was quick to leap on her reaction. "You sure you want to go through with this? It's not too late to back out."

"I'm not chickening out on Carter. He put his life on the line for me. It's the least I can do for him in return."

"He's a soldier. You're not."

"He's the man I love," she replied simply.

"All right, then. Let's go."

Chapter 15

Despite her bravado with Brady, Lily was tense. It wasn't every day a girl intentionally came as close to dying as possible without actually croaking. The way Brady explained it, his men had surrounded the cabin Carter was staying in. Without Carter's knowledge, they'd wired the place to blow up. Brady grumbled a little bit about that part of the plan. Apparently, his guys had had a difficult time sneaking up on Carter undetected. He was very good at what he did.

That made her feel better. But then Brady went on to describe the small hole his men had dug by hand under the cabin. The building supposedly sat up on cinder blocks a few feet above the ground. It allowed for more air circulation in the Southern heat, and for the occasional flood in the Louisiana bayou.

The plan was for Carter to cut a hole in the floor once she joined him in the cabin. At the last moment before the cabin blew up, she and Carter were to drop through the hole in the floor into the safety pit. Then Brady would blow up the building above them in a spectacular blast that would vaporize it and everything in it. The Russians would be given a few minutes to examine the site, then local fire department crews would be allowed to approach the blaze and put it out. Easy as pie.

Right. Easy as pie to die. But, hey, she'd asked for it.

"You still want to do this?" Brady asked quietly from the driver's seat. "The turnoff's just up ahead. Last chance to back out. Once I head down the driveway to Carter's place, the Russians will know where he is. There'll be no going back."

She took a deep breath. "Let's do it."

Truth be told, she was more worried about the next five minutes facing Carter than having to deal with the Russians whenever they decided to make their move.

Brady nodded and turned off the main road. The track, which he'd optimistically called a driveway, was a rutted strip of red clay that all but jarred her teeth out of her head as the four-wheel-drive Jeep banged and bumped its way along.

They must have driven for fifteen minutes before a tiny clearing opened up in the canopy of trees and ghostly Spanish moss.

"Let me get out first," Brady muttered. "He won't shoot me on sight." He reached for his door handle and added, "I hope."

Lily peered through the darkness at a tiny, low cabin. It had a tin roof and a porch stretching across its front that was littered with junk—a decrepit rocking chair, a wagon wheel, a small barrel, a skin of some kind stretched on a rough frame.

No lights shone through the windows. Frankly, the place looked deserted.

"Boo?" Brady called out low. "It's me, White Horse."

A shadow materialized out of the trees beyond the house. "What the hell are you doing here? Is Lily okay?"

Her heart flip-flopped to hear Carter mention her in that tone of concern.

"Funny you should ask," Brady said evenly. "She's here with me now."

Lily took that as her cue to step out of the Jeep. She walked around its front and started at the sight that greeted her. Carter was dressed in rough jeans and a ratty T-shirt, his face covered in some dark, greasy substance that made him look like a crazy Vietnam veteran. And he was cradling a nasty-looking rifle easily in his arms. She'd never seen him look so…violent. This was the soldier within him that he'd so pined for? This man was a killer.

"What. In the hell. Is she doing here?" Carter gritted out, low and angry.

"I need to talk to you, Carter. Do you have a sec?" She tried to keep her voice cheerful and light but feared she sounded like a scared-to-death mouse.

"No, actually. I don't have a sec. There's been activity around this place. I think it's compromised, Brady. I need to get out of here."

"About that. What say we step inside for a moment?" his boss replied.

Lily picked her way up the rickety steps, avoiding the spot where one was missing. Blowing up this shack was going to be no big loss at any rate.

The living room was barely bigger than a postage stamp, and the three of them hardly had room to sit down without banging knees. Carter glared at her as she perched on the edge of a rickety chair that looked like it might collapse if she sneezed.

"Carter," she said carefully, "I know you think you're doing the right thing by leaving me, but it's not the right thing for me. I know being with you could be dangerous, but I don't care."

He started to argue with her, but she cut him off.

"Brady and I have a plan. We're going to trick the Russians into thinking they've successfully killed you. Then you and I can be together and not be in any danger at all."

"What plan?" Carter snapped, none too happy. Her heart broke a little at how distant he was being with her. It was like he'd put her in a drawer and closed away all his feelings for her in it.

Brady dived in and explained.

"You brought a Russian hit team to my front steps?" Carter demanded when Brady finished talking.

Lily winced. "Well, yes. But we also brought Alpha Squad with us."

Brady added, "They're who you've seen moving around the place. They got under here this afternoon while you were out fishing and wired it to blow. They dug a pit for you two to hide in when we blow the joint, too. It's right in front of where you're sitting. All you have to do is saw a hole in the floor to get to it, and we're good to go."

"How soon do you expect this Russian hit squad to come for me?" he demanded.

"Could be an hour. Could be a couple of days," Brady replied.

"I refuse to use Lily as bait. Put her back in the Jeep and get her out of here."

Brady sighed. "No can do, bro. She's a civilian. I can't just order her around like I can you."

Carter's gaze narrowed to irritated slits. "Get out of here, Lily."

She glanced over at Brady. "Could Carter and I have a moment alone to talk?"

"Sure." Brady seemed relieved to escape the tension in the tiny space. He stepped outside and she turned to Carter.

"Why don't you want me here? Is it because you don't love me?"

He jolted. "Hell, no. It's because I do love you!"

"I happen to love you, too. Think about all those worried protective feelings you're having and realize I'm having those same feelings for you."

"Thank you, Lily. I truly appreciate it. But I'm a soldier. I'm trained to handle killers coming after me. You're not."

He wasn't going to let her do this the easy way. She took a deep breath and said quietly, "You may be trained to do this, but you can't be sure your body will always function when it needs to. I have no way of knowing you'll be able to do what you have to when the Russians attack you." It was a low blow to bring up his seizures, especially when they were so much better now. But she was willing to fight dirty to get her man.

He stared at her bleakly. "All the more reason for you to get the hell out of here."

"I'm not leaving you."

"I can't protect you," he shot back.

"Carter, I love you just the way you are. I don't care if you're Superman or not."

"Yeah, well, if someone's trying to kill you, then you need Superman. Not some screwed-up-in-the-head has-been like me."

"They're not trying to kill me. They're trying to kill

you. And besides, I'm getting sick and tired of you moping around feeling sorry for yourself because you may be done as a Special Forces soldier."

He looked startled and she pressed her momentary advantage. "Ninety-nine-point-nine percent of the male population of the United States are not trained killers. They go about their regular lives, have jobs and families and kids, and no one ever asks them to blow something up or kill someone. They live happy and fulfilling lives. What's so bad about that?"

"Nothing's bad about that. I do what I do so they can have those nice lives."

"And when is it your turn to live that life? If you were never in that firefight in Sudan, you'd still retire from this career at some point, wouldn't you?"

"Yes, but—"

"But nothing. This gig would come to an end one way or another in a few years anyway. What were you planning to do with yourself then? Commit hara-kiri?"

"No, I wasn't planning to gut myself ninja fashion."

"Then what?"

"I don't know. Maybe stick around H.O.T. Watch as an intel analyst. Continue developing software for them."

"Why can't you do that now? Move up your timetable a few years. Get on with a normal life."

"Because I've got unfinished business. I'm not entirely right in the head."

She sighed. "Is anybody who does this job for as long as you have truly right in the head?" She heard a muffled snort of laughter from the front porch. Great. Brady was listening in on this little heart-to-heart. The joys of dealing with a Special Forces team. They all seemed to know each other's business.

"Assuming I could just walk away from my work

and start a normal life, I'd still have Russians trying to kill me."

"Hence the plan to convince them you're dead and gone," she retorted.

"Then what? I assume a new identity? Move somewhere remote and isolated and expect you to drop everything in your life to join me? What about your parents, Lily? Your work? You're a brilliant scientist. You can't just walk away from all of that."

She replied drily, "They've got this thing called the internet now. Turns out I can live in one place and communicate with my colleagues and even do my research from some other place. Besides, I've decided to accept the government's offer to continue my research at H.O.T. Watch…which just happens to be remote and isolated. The perfect place for you and me to lie low for a few years."

"Dammit, Lily. I'm not good enough for you!"

"Why don't you let me be the judge of that?"

Brady's voice came through the door low and urgent. "Uh, folks, you're gonna have to continue this little drama later. We've got company inbound."

Lily's heart slammed into her throat. Apparently the Russians had decided to deal with Carter sooner rather than later.

"How long?" Carter bit out.

"Alpha Squad's perimeter man picked up movement about halfway down the drive. They're coming in on foot. Twenty minutes maybe."

Carter looked around frantically. "Dammit, there's no place to hide you!"

"Like it or not, we're in this together now," she declared. Her tummy flip-flopped at the realization that she could die—they could both die—in just a few minutes.

"Well, I like it not," he snapped.

"Shouldn't we get busy sawing that hole in the floor?" she suggested.

He threw her a furious look and grabbed an ax out of the corner. After several mighty swings, he created a slit in the wood planks of the flooring. Picking up a rusty saw, he poked it through the slit and started hauling up and down on the tool furiously. She supposed that, if nothing else, making the hole would give him a chance to work out some of his anger at her for getting him into this mess.

"What can I do to help?" she asked.

"Find all the blankets you can and soak them with water. We'll need insulation from the heat of the blast and the fire to follow."

She scavenged both rooms of the cabin and came up with two ratty quilts and a heavy boiled wool blanket with only a few moth holes in it. She headed for the rusty sink and the sulfur-smelling water coming from its tap.

"How's the hole coming?" Brady asked from the porch a few minutes later.

"One more side to go," Carter grunted.

"I'm gonna have to head for the woods now," Brady replied. "You've got maybe five minutes before you need to be in position. And here, I brought these for you two."

The door slipped open and Lily took the two bulky items he shoved through at her. The door closed again and she heard a single faint footstep as Brady faded away into the night. These Special Forces types were freaky quiet.

Carter made a vaguely amused sound when he saw what she held.

"What are these?"

"Bulletproof vests. Put one on under your T-shirt."

She did as he told her without comment, stripping off

her navy-blue T-shirt, donning the surprisingly light vest, and then yanking her shirt back down over the additional bulk.

Carter stood up, observing his work critically. "I've left just enough wood intact to keep the floor from dropping out right now. All we have to do is jump on the boards and we'll fall right through the hole."

"Now what?"

"Now you and I should probably start a loud argument to convince the Russians I'm distracted and an easy target."

"Should you light a lamp and stand in front of the window or something?"

He answered without even a trace of humor. "They'll have infrared scopes."

"Which means what?" she asked.

"Which means they'll see our heat signatures through the walls and shoot me through the wood without bothering to wait for me to stand in front of a window."

Panic ripped through her. She'd had no idea they'd be *this* exposed to the killers.

"Oh, now she gets what I've been trying to tell her," he groused loudly.

She looked at him, startled. He gave her an encouraging nod. "Yeah, well, I can't help it if I'm a lousy civilian and I don't understand all this stupid military stuff you keep talking about," she declared back.

"You're going to get us both killed!"

"That's what you get for never bothering to talk to me in plain English. It's not my fault if you use all that lingo and fancy military terminology. If you weren't so busy trying to impress me all the time with how macho and sexy you are, maybe we wouldn't be in this situation!"

Carter grinned at the reference to being sexy. He yelled back that she was a sex maniac and how could he have known she was a groupie for soldiers until they'd gotten together.

She laughed under her breath and yelled at him about never letting her wear the nice clothes she bought, and he complained that she was too high-maintenance a woman with no common sense.

He got up and started pacing.

In between yelling about how he never did any work around the house, she whispered, "Why are you moving around?"

"If I make the shot too easy, their sniper may get suspicious," he muttered back, before going on a diatribe about her leaving her telescopes and computer printouts all over the place.

She was perplexed when he looped his hands behind the back of his head and let his elbows drift forward over his ears. And then it hit her. He was trying to make sure the sniper shot at his bulletproof-vested body and not his head. Her blood ran cold.

"I can't believe I came all this way to see you again. I forgot what a colossal jerk you are!"

"And I forgot what a total bitch you are! I don't care how good the sex was. It's not worth having to put up with this!"

She stuck her tongue out at him over that one. Great. Just what she needed all his teammates to hear—that they'd had wild monkey sex together. She'd never look Brady Hathaway in the eye again.

Bang! Bang!

Carter exhaled in a whoosh and dropped like a rock to the floor.

Lily screamed her head off, and it was no act. She dived on top of him. "Oh, God, oh, God. Are you hurt? Where are you hit?" Panic choked her until she could hardly breathe. "What am I supposed to do? Carter, you can't die on me!"

"I'll live," he gritted out between clenched teeth in a whisper. "Forgot how hard high-caliber slugs hit. Scream some more."

It was no stretch to scream his name and beg him not to die on her. And then something horrifying dawned on her. Brady had said to give it one minute after Carter was shot and then to jump into the pit so he could blow up the house.

That minute was about up.

"It's time to go," she murmured between rants about him always leaving her like this.

"Small problem. I can't move," he muttered back.

Oh, no. Not now.

Chapter 16

Carter's ribs felt as if he'd just been hit by twin sledge-hammers. Lily was doing a so-believable-it-had-to-be-real job of freaking out beside him, and he'd just finished counting to sixty in his head. And every muscle in his body was starting to clench up.

"Help me roll over to the hole," he muttered.

"Right. Good idea," she blurted. Her hands were on him then, shoving and tugging. Brave Lily. She just saw what had to be done and dived in. No fear. No second thoughts.

She loved the same way. Bravely. Fearlessly. He was a hell of a lucky man. And as he thought about her and all the joy she'd brought to his life, the strangest thing happened. His muscle spasms unwound. Not enough to run around in the woods and play commando. But enough to move after a fashion. Enough to sit up beside the hole.

Enough to mutter to her, "Shout about all the blood."

She complied in a shriek that left him partially deaf, "Oh, my GOD! There's blood everywhere! What am I supposed to do? You're going to bleed to death! Water. I've got to boil water. Sterilize some of this garbage and make you bandages. Yes, that's it."

He frowned up at her in the gloom of the darkened cabin. What was she up to?

And then she moved over to the tiny propane stove and he saw her logic. An explanation for the explosion about to happen.

"Lily," he managed weakly. "Stop that. I'm a goner already. You can't save me."

"Noooo!" she keened convincingly.

She scooped up the armloads of blankets and rushed over to him, dropping hard to her knees beside him…right on top of the floorboards. She grabbed the front of his shirt as the planks gave way and he flung himself into the hole after her. He'd barely cleared the floorboards and was still falling when the first flash of light—the detonation cord blowing—illuminated.

He landed hard on top of Lily as the second, main explosion detonated. The world went white, then black; loud, then silent. And then hot. So hot he thought his back was going to burst into flames. He imagined the skin blackening and peeling away from his raw flesh. Then Lily was wriggling beneath him. He rolled aside in the tight confines of the pit and she flung the wet blankets over them.

Lying on his side, he spied something useful. He murmured, "Rebreather units. Brady thought of everything."

He passed one to Lily and they jammed the pair of tiny portable oxygen units into each of their mouths. He lacked fine motor control, but he was able to drag the Mylar blanket Alpha Squad had left for them across Lily and himself. The high-tech material would reflect massive amounts of heat. Hopefully enough to keep them from roasting down here.

"How long?" Lily gasped.

"Few minutes," he gasped back. The heat was incredible. It felt like they were being baked in an oven. Intellectually, he knew Alpha Squad had blown up the cabin with shaped charges that directed most of the force of the blast outward, away from their hiding spot. Ideally, most of the cabin was blown out and away from them, too, minimizing the amount of debris burning on top of them now. At least that would have been the plan.

Lily's arms crept around his waist, and he put his arms around her as well.

"I love you, Carter," she murmured around the mouth breathing unit.

"I love you, too."

She took her unit out long enough to say, "I'm sorry I messed up all your plans for noble sacrifice, but I just couldn't let you go. I hope you'll forgive me, but after we saved the world, I just had to save ours, too."

He chuckled, startled that his chest muscles were already easing up enough to allow for that. He reached up and took out his unit to reply, "If this is your idea of saving someone, I'd hate to see your idea of messing someone up."

"It is a little extreme, isn't it?"

"Just a bit."

They waited for several endless minutes and then he heard a noise that made his heart sing. A big, noisy engine rumbling toward them. Like a fire truck. Within minutes, hot water began to drip in around the edges of the Mylar blanket. He adjusted their wet quilts to catch the runoff as the fire crew put out the blaze overhead. The air around them cooled noticeably and they were able to take their breathing units out entirely.

Lily wasted no time picking up their conversation where they'd left off. "Forgive me?"

He smiled down at her. "How can I not? I love you and I want nothing more on this Earth than to be with you."

"Even if you have to give up being a commando?"

"I think that ship has sailed. I'm done with that phase of my life." The knowing sank into him as deep as the heat and fury of the fire above them had. But shockingly, he was calm inside. At peace, even. Lily was right. He knew being an operator couldn't go on forever. But he had an outstanding education and Brady had already asked him to continue working with H.O.T. Watch when he retired from the field. Life would go on. He got that now, thanks to Lily.

"This was a crazy scheme, you know," he murmured. "Did you have to blow us up?"

She shrugged. "You love me because I'm a little bit nuts. I think outside the box."

He laughed. "That's a word for it."

"You won't mind having to lie low at H.O.T. Watch and live like a recluse?" she mumbled against his chest.

"Not if you won't."

"Will we be together?" she asked.

"Forever. I promise. Mr. and Mrs. John Doe."

She was silent for a moment. He waited her out, holding his breath in tense anticipation. Finally, belatedly, her body went rigid against his. "Mr. and Mrs. Doe?" she echoed.

"You know, for a brilliant astrophysicist, you sure can be slow on the uptake, kid."

Her voice rose on a note of excitement. "Are you asking me to marry you?"

"What do you think, Einstein? Of course I am."

"Oh." A pause. "Oh!"

"Well?" he demanded.

"Well, what?"

"Well, what do you say? Will you?"

Just then their blanket ripped away from them. Alarmed, he rolled on top of Lily protectively.

"You two okay?" a firefighter in full gear asked from above them.

Carter handed Lily up to the guy and then climbed to his feet, as well. They picked their way carefully through the black and smoking debris.

Brady came over to join them. "Good to see you two in one piece. Alpha Squad reported that the Russians bugged out when they heard the sirens. Alpha's trailing them back to New Orleans as we speak."

Lily turned into Carter's chest, and his arms came up around her.

She started to shake. Alarmed, he tilted his head down to see if she was crying. But the shaking increased, and in the faint glow of the firelight still seeping around the edges of their protective shell, he saw she was laughing.

"We did it. We fooled them!"

"You're okay then?" he asked.

"Of course I'm okay."

He paused. Then he took a deep breath and dived in. "And about what I asked before? Will you marry me?"

"For a soldier, you can be pretty dense sometimes," she declared. "You think I led a hit squad to us, let your boss blow up a building around us, and hid beneath a burning blaze with you, and I *don't* want to marry you?"

Joy exploded in his heart, and without warning the remaining tension in his muscles released. All of it. All at once. Gone. He'd found the trigger that would release his freeze-ups. Lily. And love.

He had no illusions that he would get better overnight, or even that the spasms would ever go away entirely. But with her help and her love, he had faith he could learn to control them and live with their remnants. He drew her up against him and kissed her with all the profound relief and bone-deep happiness in his soul.

"Promise me one thing," he murmured against her smiling lips.

"Anything."

"You'll finally get around to wearing that red teddy on our wedding night."

"You've got a deal, Carter Baigneaux. You've got a deal."

* * * * *

COMING NEXT MONTH

Available March 29, 2011

ROMANTIC SUSPENSE

SRSCNM0311

REQUEST YOUR FREE BOOKS!

2 FREE NOVELS PLUS 2 FREE GIFTS!

Silhouette®

ROMANTIC SUSPENSE

Sparked by Danger, Fueled by Passion.

YES! Please send me 2 FREE Silhouette® Romantic Suspense novels and my 2 FREE gifts (gifts are worth about $10). After receiving them, if I don't wish to receive any more books, I can return the shipping statement marked "cancel." If I don't cancel, I will receive 4 brand-new novels every month and be billed just $4.24 per book in the U.S. or $4.99 per book in Canada. That's a saving of at least 15% off the cover price! It's quite a bargain! Shipping and handling is just 50¢ per book in the U.S. and 75¢ per book in Canada.* I understand that accepting the 2 free books and gifts places me under no obligation to buy anything. I can always return a shipment and cancel at any time. Even if I never buy another book, the two free books and gifts are mine to keep forever.

240/340 SDN FC95

Name	(PLEASE PRINT)

Address	Apt. #

City	State/Prov.	Zip/Postal Code

Signature (if under 18, a parent or guardian must sign)

Mail to the **Reader Service:**

IN U.S.A.: P.O. Box 1867, Buffalo, NY 14240-1867
IN CANADA: P.O. Box 609, Fort Erie, Ontario L2A 5X3

Not valid for current subscribers to Silhouette Romantic Suspense books.

Want to try two free books from another line?
Call 1-800-873-8635 or visit www.ReaderService.com.

* Terms and prices subject to change without notice. Prices do not include applicable taxes. Sales tax applicable in N.Y. Canadian residents will be charged applicable taxes. Offer not valid in Quebec. This offer is limited to one order per household. All orders subject to credit approval. Credit or debit balances in a customer's account(s) may be offset by any other outstanding balance owed by or to the customer. Please allow 4 to 6 weeks for delivery. Offer available while quantities last.

Your Privacy—The Reader Service is committed to protecting your privacy. Our Privacy Policy is available online at www.ReaderService.com or upon request from the Reader Service.

We make a portion of our mailing list available to reputable third parties that offer products we believe may interest you. If you prefer that we not exchange your name with third parties, or if you wish to clarify or modify your communication preferences, please visit us at www.ReaderService.com/consumerschoice or write to us at Reader Service Preference Service, P.O. Box 9062, Buffalo, NY 14269. Include your complete name and address.

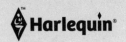

Harlequin®

ROMANTIC
SUSPENSE

Sparked by Danger, Fueled by Passion

SAME GREAT STORIES
AND AUTHORS!

Starting April 2011,
Silhouette Romantic Suspense will
become Harlequin Romantic Suspense,
but rest assured that this series will
continue to be the ultimate destination
for sweeping romance and heart-racing
suspense with the same great authors
you've come to know and love!

SRSHARLEQUIN11

Selene wanted nothing to do with the father of her son, Alex; but Aristedes had other plans...that included them.

Read on for an sneak peek from
THE SARANTOS SECRET BABY by Olivia Gates,
available April 2011, only from Harlequin Desire.

"You were right to turn my marriage offer down," Aristedes said.

And Selene found her voice at last, found the words that would not betray the blow he'd dealt her. "Thanks for letting me know. You didn't have to come all the way here, though. You could have just let it go. I left yesterday with the understanding that this case is closed."

Before the hot needles behind her eyes could dissolve into an unforgivable display of stupidity and weakness, she began to close the door.

The door stopped against an immovable object. His flat palm.

"I can't accept that." His voice was low, leashed.

What did her tormentor mean now? Was he ending one game only to start another?

She raised eyes as bruised as her self-respect to his, found nothing there but solemnity and determination.

Before she could voice her confusion, he elaborated. "I never let anything go unless I'm certain it's unworkable. I realize I made you an unworkable offer, and that's why I'm withdrawing it. I'm here to offer something else. A workability study."

She leaned against the door, thankful for its support and partial shield. "Your son and I are not a business venture you can test for feasibility."

His gaze grew deeper, made her feel as if he was trying to delve into her mind, take control of it. "It's actually the other way around. I'm the one who would be tested."

She shook her head. "Why bother? I know—and *you* know—you're not workable. Not with me."

His spectacular eyebrows lowered over eyes she felt were emitting silver hypnosis. "You're right again. Neither you nor I have any reason to believe that isn't the truth. The only truth. It might be best for both you and Alex to never hear from me again, to forget I exist. But then again, maybe not. I'm only asking for the chance for both of us to find out for certain. You believe I'm unworkable in any personal relationship. I've lived my life based on that belief about myself. I never really had reason to question it. But I have one now. In fact, I have two."

Find out what happens in
THE SARANTOS SECRET BABY by Olivia Gates,
available April 2011, only from Harlequin Desire.

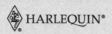

SPECIAL EDITION

Life, Love, Family and Top Authors!

In April, Harlequin Special Edition features
four *USA TODAY* bestselling authors!

FORTUNE'S JUST DESSERTS
by *MARIE FERRARELLA*

Follow the latest drama featuring the ever-powerful
and passionate Fortune family.

YOURS, MINE & OURS
by *JENNIFER GREEN*

Life can't get any more chaotic for Amanda Scott.
Divorced and a single mom, Amanda had given up on
the knight-in-shining-armor fairy tale until a friendship
with Mike becomes something a little more....

THE BRIDE PLAN (*SECOND-CHANCE BRIDAL* MINISERIES)
by *KASEY MICHAELS*

Finding love and second chances for others is
second nature for bridal-shop owner Chessie.
But will *she* finally get her second chance?

THE RANCHER'S DANCE
by *ALLISON LEIGH*

Return to the Double C Ranch this month—where love, loss
and new beginnings set the stage for Allison Leigh's latest title.

*Look for these titles and others in April 2011
from Harlequin Special Edition, wherever books are sold.*

❖ Harlequin®

A *Romance* FOR EVERY MOOD™

www.eHarlequin.com